The
Mystery
of the
Indian Carvings

Gloria Repp

The Mystery of the Indian Carvings

Contents

The *Sea Star*

Where was the ferry? It should have been here an hour ago—what could have happened to it? Julie stared at the handful of boats moored nearby, tempted to shout her question into the cool, salty air.

For the hundredth time, she searched the maze of islands that dotted the shimmering blue ocean.

For sure, one of those must be Bartlett Island! Aunt Myra and Uncle Nate lived there, and they'd said she could take the ferry.

An elderly man shuffled past, giving her a bright, inquisitive glance, and she pretended not to see him.

She sat down on her upended suitcase, smoothed out the worried frown from her forehead, and tried to look unconcerned. After all, this wasn't the first time she'd traveled alone. Her big brother had teased her about being a "seasoned traveler" when she went out to visit him in Texas.

1

This trip was different. She crumpled a pleat in the blue skirt her stepmom had insisted she wear. This time, she wasn't going to be met by a fond older brother. She didn't even know these relatives she'd been sent to visit, but no matter what happened, she had to get along with them.

"You'll do fine, Julie. I know I'll be proud of you," her father had said. He'd waved cheerfully as she boarded the bus in Victoria for the short ride up the island.

Vancouver Island was part of Canada, but it didn't seem as foreign as she'd pictured it. From the bus, the small towns they passed looked the same as most towns in the United States.

The bus driver had been kind. When she got off the bus at Chemainus, he'd told her that the town used to be an Indian village, and he pointed out the ferry dock. "Right down that hill, Miss," he said, and she noticed his Canadian accent.

Sure enough, the gravel road sloped toward the ocean, and it took her to the dock and a sign with red-painted letters: *Chemainus Ferry.*

She jerked upright as an explosion of sound broke the stillness, but it was only a speedboat, streaking out of the sleepy little harbor. Oily green waves slapped against the pilings of the dock and flattened into slow, rhythmic swells that ticked away the seconds, one by one.

What if the ferry didn't come? What would she do tonight?

Farther along the shore, a weather-beaten shack leaned into the hillside. Over its door hung a handwritten sign: BAIT. That's where the old man had gone. Maybe someone in there would know about the ferry.

She picked up her suitcase, a new blue one that Dad had bought her, and hauled it along the road to the shack. Fortunately, her trunk had already been shipped ahead. Anything else she needed would be sent later, if she could stay.

If she could stay.

She scuffed through the gravel, angry again. Why had her stepmom been so sure that she'd cause trouble on Bartlett Island? According to *her,* Julie should go to one of those horrible summer camps for problem girls, the kind where you lived in tents or something for months and months.

If it weren't for Dad, she'd be on her way to one right now.

She pushed past a sagging screen door and blinked in the store's cool, fishy-smelling gloom.

The old man behind the cash register peered over his glasses. "I was just about to come out and ask if you got a problem," he said. "Been sitting there a long time, eh?" He definitely sounded like a Canadian.

She made her voice dignified. "I'm waiting for the ferry to Bartlett Island."

"Oh-ho, the ferry? Well now, you do have a problem." The bait man pushed his glasses up onto his forehead and scratched his sparse gray hair. "Ferry schedule's been changed, and I'll bet you didn't know that. Yep, that's the way it is with them government boys. They keep changing things around to suit themselves."

He unfolded a yellow sheet of paper. "Let's see. Ferry goes to Bartlett on Mondays and Fridays. This being Tuesday, of course—no ferry."

"But they sent us a schedule, and it shows Tuesdays and Thursdays!"

"Now don't get upset," the old man said. "Happens all the time. Them government boys . . . We'll take a look and see if someone can run you across." He strolled to the doorway and peered out. "Nobody around."

She almost said, "So I noticed!" but she clamped her mouth shut.

"I'll be right back—don't go away," he said over his shoulder.

She leaned against the counter and eyed the ferry schedule. She certainly wasn't going anywhere. Not back to Chicago, to a stepmom who didn't want her getting in the way.

Her hand strayed to the necklace Dad had given her. He'd told her she had a cousin here, only a year older. Karin.

Maybe Karin was waiting for her at the ferry dock on Bartlett Island.

Her heart lifted. Maybe Karin would turn out to be like Melissa, her best friend back at home. No, nobody could be like Melissa. But maybe she and Karin could do things together, and Karin would tell her about the Indians—

4

"Hey, you must be Julie. " A cheerful voice rang out, and a tall blond teenager followed the bait man inside.

"Looks like you weren't forgot, after all," the old man said with a chuckle. "Stan's come over for you."

"That's right," Stan said. "Your Uncle Nate asked me to pick you up."

Before Julie could answer, an indignant voice exclaimed, "What kind of service is this anyway?"

A blond young woman, trimly dressed in green, marched up to the cash register.

She frowned at the dusty countertop and frowned at the old man. "Where is that Bartlett Island ferry? It's over an hour late. I can't sit in this backwater all day."

The old man's grin faded. "Ferry schedule changed, ma'am. Not my fault." He glanced at the teenager. "Stan, seein' as you're taking the young lady over to Bartlett, maybe you wouldn't mind another passenger, eh?"

"That would help." The woman turned to Stan and flashed him a smile. "I'd appreciate it."

Stan blinked at her with a dazzled expression. "Sure, no problem." He picked up Julie's suitcase and headed for the door. "Let's get going."

Julie thanked the bait man with a smile and followed Stan outside, glad to get back into the June sunlight. The blond woman came too, her quick footsteps crunching on the gravel.

"Your uncle had an emergency call," Stan said. He waited for Julie to catch up. "The man who runs

5

the general store on Bartlett fell and cut himself pretty bad. They called your uncle, even though he's not really doctoring anymore."

She accepted the news in silence. At least her uncle had wanted to come and pick her up.

She glanced sideways at Stan. He might be a couple of years older, and he looked as if he spent a lot of time outside. She liked his freckles and curly blond hair. Bartlett Island might be fun with Stan around.

At the dock, he leaped into a long white boat, set down Julie's suitcase, and turned with a grin. "Welcome aboard the *Sea Star,* ladies."

Julie took a reluctant step forward. The boat rose and fell in an unsettling way. How was she supposed to get into it without losing her balance and falling into a disgraceful heap?

Stan stretched out a hand, and she grabbed it.

She lunged into the boat, dropped onto the nearest seat, and hung on. The *Sea Star* was larger than some of the other boats, but it still looked awfully small to go out on the ocean.

The blond woman stepped in with ease and sat across from her. "I think we'd better get acquainted," she said with a smile. "I'm Vivian Taylor, and you're—?"

"Julie Fletcher." The woman must have decided to be friendly.

Vivian Taylor cocked her head at Stan and smiled her question.

"I'm Stan Caldwell," he said. "*Sea Star* here is the mission boat." He patted it affectionately. "My parents work for the mission on Bartlett, and I help around the place."

"A mission! That's interesting," Vivian Taylor said. "You'll have to tell me all about it. I'm a writer, and I'm going to do a magazine article about your island. Is it a Catholic mission, like on the other islands?"

Stan started the engine and raised his voice above its noise. "I don't think so," he said. "Mrs. Warner and her husband settled on Bartlett a long time ago. They built a church for the Indians and did some medical work too."

He guided the boat out into open water. "Since her husband died, Mrs. Warner just keeps up with the summer camp and church work. Some of the Indians work on her farm."

Julie found that she enjoyed the thrust of the boat skimming across the water, and she relaxed her grip. She lifted her face to the salty breeze that rushed through her hair.

Stan had pointed the boat toward a cluster of islands, and she studied them expectantly. Some were larger than others, but they all seemed alike, with rocky shores and prickly-looking green trees.

"That's Kuper Island," Stan said, waving to the left. "And that big one over there is Saltspring. Sometimes we go there on bike trips, or else we go to Chemainus and down to Victoria."

He glanced at Julie. "You're from the States, aren't you? How did you come?"

7

"Dad and I flew from Chicago to Seattle, then to Victoria," she said. "I didn't realize there were so many islands around here."

"We've got a bunch of them. There's Bartlett now—way over there with the long point."

He looked at Vivian Taylor, who was writing in a small notebook. "You can tell your readers it was named after Captain John Bartlett, an American sea captain who explored around here a couple hundred years ago. He was probably hunting sea-otter pelts, like everyone else."

Julie gazed at the curving edge of Bartlett Island as it drew close. Her heart beat faster, and she stopped listening to Stan.

If her relatives were anything like Dad, she'd be okay. Her stepmom was the only person she had trouble getting along with—Barbara, with her red hair and her pert way of doing things that Dad thought was so cute.

Now Stan was pointing out the small settlement ahead of them. "See that red brick building? That's the mission. The little white one is the church, and that long pier is where the ferry docks."

He glanced at Julie. "You'd like our church," he said. "We've got quite a bunch of kids there, and we have fun when we get together. Maybe you can get your uncle to bring you on Sunday"

"I'll try." Julie smiled to herself, remembering how church used to seem pretty boring.

Vivian Taylor interrupted her thoughts with an excited little squeal. "Oh, yes, of course! Your uncle must be Dr. Fletcher!"

Julie shifted uncomfortably, hoping she wouldn't have to answer questions about a relative she didn't know, but the woman went right on. "I've heard that he's a most unusual and talented man, and he's got a house full of Indian artifacts. I'd love to get an interview with him."

While she was wondering how to answer, Stan said, "I'll take you right over to the Fletchers' dock, Julie."

He swung the boat past a rocky point with only one house and turned down the other side of the island into a quiet cove. The boat's engine slowed to a purr as they approached a small floating dock.

Vivian Taylor gathered up her notebook and an expensive-looking camera. "Oh, I want to get off here too," she exclaimed. "It would be perfect!"

"No, you don't." Stan shook his head at her, his face serious. "Dr. Fletcher hates to be disturbed. And he doesn't like visitors. He won't even allow a telephone in the house."

Vivian Taylor frowned and sank back into her seat, but she took pictures of the shoreline while Stan eased the boat up against the dock. Again Julie was glad for Stan's steadying hand as she stepped from the boat onto the shifting wooden platform.

He carried her suitcase along the dock toward a path that disappeared into the trees.

As they reached the path, he turned to her. "Don't be surprised if things here seem a little unusual," he murmured. "Some people say the Fletchers are peculiar. I haven't figured them out yet myself, but if you need a friend, I'll be around."

Julie bit her lip. What was that all about?

He glanced toward the trees and added, "Looks like your aunt's on her way to meet you. See ya later."

He sent her a grin and turned back to his boat.

A Missing Raven

Julie watched the thin woman stepping carefully down the path. Her narrow face and pale blue eyes looked worried, and her stiff little smile held no welcome.

"Hello, Julie," she said. "It's nice to see you at last." Her voice was high and clear, the Canadian accent crisp.

"The ferry . . ."

"Yes, I'm sorry about that," her aunt said. "We've had a terrible day here, with your uncle being called away just when he was coming over to pick you up. I suppose it took Karin a while to get over to the mission and give Stan the message."

She brushed back wisps of faded blond hair that had escaped from a knot on top of her head. "With the raven missing and all, it's been most upsetting." She sighed and turned toward the rocky path. "Let's go up to the house."

11

Puzzled, Julie picked up her suitcase and trudged after her, up the hill and through giant cedar trees. The brown house was set snugly into the hillside, and something about its peaked roof reminded her of a Swiss chalet.

Aunt Myra sighed again as she opened a door that led into the kitchen.

Julie followed her inside, put down her suitcase, and met the cool gaze of a blond girl who sat at the counter.

"Well, Karin, here's your cousin Julie," Aunt Myra said.

Julie tried a friendly smile.

The girl's blue eyes slid over her in a long, measuring look. "Hi."

She tilted her glass of milk to finish it and stood up. "Have to run—" She tossed back her gleaming hair and walked off.

"Karin will be back in a little while." Aunt Myra sounded embarrassed. "I'm sure you girls will have a good time getting to know each other."

She led Julie through the kitchen to a hall paneled in honey-colored wood and up a curving flight of stairs.

Julie reached the top of the steps just in time to see a door to her left closing silently. Was that Karin's room? Her aunt turned to the right, walked past a bathroom and another closed door, then paused in front of the last door and opened it.

"This is your room," she said. "I hope you like it."

"Oh, yes!" Julie exclaimed, gazing at the soft blue curtains and thick rug. Heavy blue drapes covered one whole wall at the far end of the room.

Aunt Myra waved her hand at a row of empty bookshelves under the window. "I didn't put out any books because I don't know what kind you like, but we have a whole library downstairs. You may take anything you want from it."

"Thank you," Julie said. The blue chair beside the shelves seemed like a good place to curl up and read.

Aunt Myra glanced at her watch. "Supper will be ready in twenty minutes, so I'd better get down to the kitchen." Her small mouth pressed itself into something like a smile, and she left.

Julie closed the door and leaned against it. Not much of a welcoming committee, were they?

She ignored a flutter of disappointment and looked around. Such a pretty room! She'd have books, too. She could count on them whenever she felt miserable.

The small bed with its soft white comforter looked cozy and inviting. She tossed her jacket onto the chair, kicked off her shoes, and flopped down onto the bed to sort out the bewilderment inside her.

Aunt Myra had seemed glad to see her. Hadn't she?

And Karin? Perhaps Karin had been . . . in a hurry. After all, this new cousin was a stranger, and Karin would have her own friends.

She rolled over and squeezed her eyes shut to block out the memory of Karin's cool stare. She thought about the happy stories Dad told her about Bartlett Island, about the Indians, and all the adventures he'd had during the summers he'd spent visiting his cousin Nate.

She sat up and pushed back her long brown hair, her fingers catching in its tangles. Dad had talked the most about Uncle Nate. He sounded like a wonderful person, and she could hardly wait to meet him.

Sounds from the kitchen below reminded her that supper would soon be ready. She checked her watch and hunted in her suitcase for a hairbrush. Only ten minutes. She'd better not be late.

Suppertime turned out to be a disappointment because her uncle didn't join them. Apparently he was still out taking care of the injured man. Karin arrived promptly and sat down with a chilly glance in Julie's direction.

At first, Aunt Myra asked questions about her family and her home in Chicago. She answered them shyly, wishing she could ask questions of her own, but soon her aunt murmured something about the missing raven and returned to her thoughts in a way that shut out conversation.

The woman looked ancient, even though she couldn't be much older than Dad. Her skin was marked with anxious lines, and a frown creased her forehead. What was she was so worried about?

The meal dragged on. Karin gave her attention to the roast beef and baked potatoes without saying anything, and for once, Julie didn't feel hungry. As soon as she dared, she excused herself from the table and slipped up to her room.

She might as well unpack, since her trunk stood in a corner of the room, waiting, and she was stuck here for three weeks anyway. Dad was planning to stop at Bartlett on his way back from his lectures in San Francisco, and that's when the grownups would discuss her.

She'd find out whether she could stay for the rest of the summer—or be sent away to camp.

Did she really want to stay here, anyway? Her fingers closed on the small figure that swung from a chain around her neck. She dropped into the blue chair and took off the pendant to admire it once more.

On the plane from Chicago, her father had presented her with a narrow box wrapped in gold paper. Inside, she'd found a strange little animal carved out of glossy brown wood. Its tiny pointed ears and face reminded her of a kitten. It seemed to be lying on its back, sleeping, with its forepaws curled over its chest.

"Oh! What's this?" she had asked.

"It's a sea otter," he said. "A water animal, like a big muskrat, but it has flippers, like a seal. See the flippers?" He pointed to what she'd thought was a wide tail, curving gracefully over the small body.

Her father smiled. "A memento of my days on beautiful Bartlett Island. I had it put on that gold

15

chain so you could wear it. I hope you'll have as many wonderful things to remember as I do."

What she remembered now, as she held the small otter in her hand, was the unhappiness she'd often seen on Dad's face. Sure, she'd caused it by her furious outbursts at home, but things didn't used to be that way. In the long years since her mother had died, she and her brother and her father got along fine. Until he met Barbara.

She jumped up, opened the window, and leaned out over the sill. Everything was turning velvety black, quite different from the brightness of a Chicago night. Through the trees nearby drifted a fresh, piney scent, mixed with a sweeter fragrance. Something must be blooming out there, and maybe she could find it tomorrow.

What else would tomorrow bring? Loneliness rushed in, threatening to smother her.

If only Melissa were here! She'd say something like, "Don't let 'em get you down!"

Julie took a ragged breath and turned from the window. Let tomorrow come. For Dad's sake, she would fit in, even though it looked as if she was going to be miserable.

In bed at last, staring into the darkness, she remembered what Stan had told her. Why had he warned her about strange things in this house?

She puzzled sleepily over Aunt Myra's missing raven. A raven was like a big black crow, right? Had the family pet disappeared? Was that why Aunt Myra acted so upset?

Maybe tomorrow she'd find out.

Thump-thud. Thump-thud. Julie snapped awake, blinked in the morning sunlight, and sat up.

Thump-thud. Thump-thud.

What in the world was that noise?

Softly muffled, it seemed to repeat itself again and again from some place nearby. Was this part of the strangeness that Stan talked about?

She had started to ease back under her blankets when she heard a slurping, watery sound through the open window. Curious, she slid out of bed and hurried to see what it was.

Through the branches, she caught sight of a large dog thirstily lapping water from a pan. His powerful muscles rippled under short black fur that gleamed in the sunlight, and she smiled at the sight of him. A black Labrador Retriever!

Besides books, she liked dogs best, even better than people. She'd never been allowed to have one, but she had pored over her brother's dog book for hours, sharing his interest.

Would this black Lab be as friendly as the book said? She'd go down right away and get to know him.

Hurriedly she dressed in new jeans—and the pink-striped blouse to give her courage—and tiptoed down the polished stairway.

The thumps had stopped, and the house lay silent around her. Something gave her the feeling that she should step softly and make as little noise as possible in the wood-paneled hall . . . as if the house itself would be displeased with any happy sounds she made.

17

Through tall glass doors, she glimpsed a room lined with bookshelves. That must be the library, but she couldn't stop to explore it now.

She stepped into the kitchen and paused. Aunt Myra was hunched over a cup of tea and Karin sat at the other end of the counter, eating a dish of oatmeal.

Breakfast time already? She'd have to visit the dog later.

Aunt Myra gave her a pale smile and waved toward the stove. "Help yourself to porridge and whatever else you'd like," she said in a blurred voice.

Julie served up a small bowl of oatmeal, poured herself a glass of milk, and sat down next to her aunt. "I saw a beautiful black Lab outside," she said. "What's his name?"

Aunt Myra put her hand to her forehead as if the effort of speaking were too much to bear. Her eyes were shadowed with dark smudges, and her face was sickly white.

Karin spoke up, but she sounded as if she were explaining something to a child. "His name is Siem. It's an Indian name."

At Julie's questioning look, she added, "If you want to know what it means, you'll have to ask Robert—he's the smart one around here."

Who was Robert?

But concern for her aunt pushed the question away. "Are you sick, Aunt Myra?" Julie asked.

"I've got one of my headaches, a migraine." Her hand moved in a feeble gesture. "I wish we could

18

find that raven club. It's a valuable part of your uncle's art collection. I can't imagine what could have happened to it."

Karin stood up and clattered her dishes into the sink.

Aunt Myra raised her voice plaintively as Karin walked out of the kitchen. "Now, listen, you girls be good." She looked at Julie. "Your uncle insists on absolute quiet in this house. He does very important work."

Julie nodded. She'd better not ask any more questions. Silently she finished her breakfast and put her dishes in the sink next to Karin's.

A door from the kitchen led into the dining room, and she wandered past a long polished table toward a fireplace with brown leather chairs arranged around it.

She turned a corner of the L-shaped room and found herself in the library. Nearest her were shelves of wooden carvings, with photographs of animals and ocean scenes arranged between them.

Exclaiming in delight, she stepped closer to study the photo of a sleek brown otter floating on his back. He seemed to be asleep, like the little carved one Dad had given her.

"Cute, huh?" Karin walked over to stand beside Julie in front of the shelves. "These are only a few of my father's Indian artifacts," she said, with a proud lift of her chin.

She slanted a glance at Julie. "If you like otters, you should see the one upstairs. It's carved out of wood and has the neatest little pointed ears. I'll show you, if you like."

Julie looked at her uncertainly, but Karin, her eyes bright, gave no hint of what she might be thinking. She hadn't seemed very friendly last night. What had changed? Maybe she just wanted to show off her father's collection.

An Indian club on the shelf attracted her notice, and she touched the gleaming wood with careful fingers. Its handle was skillfully shaped to ensure a secure grip, and the other end was carved into the snarling head of a bear.

She looked at Karin. "That raven club Aunt Myra was talking about—is it like this one?"

"Yeah. Except that it looks like a raven." Karin sounded curt again. "C'mon, I'll show you that sea otter."

"Okay." Could there be another one like hers?

Karin marched into the hall, bounded lightly up the stairs, and stopped at the room next to Julie's.

Its door stood slightly ajar, and her cousin pushed it wide open, motioning Julie to enter.

Miniature totem poles with sly-looking animal faces grinned at her from shelves by the fireplace.

Beside them squatted a beaver with a face like a bulldog's, his long teeth bared to protect the bowl that was carved into his back.

Where was the otter?

Another shelf held woven baskets with intricate zigzag designs. A cone-shaped hat lay next to them, and she picked it up for a closer look.

Only then did she realize that a large desk, scattered with papers, stood nearby.

Was this someone's office? She turned to ask Karin.

A door opened at the far end of the room, and a tall, dark-haired man carrying a camera walked up to the desk.

He stared at her, and Julie dropped the hat back onto the shelf. She looked up into steel-blue eyes set in a frowning face.

Exploring

"What are you doing here?" he asked.

Julie darted a frightened glance over her shoulder. But her cousin was gone.

"I—I didn't mean to . . ." The words stuck in her throat.

"You must be Julie," he said, and the frown lifted from his black eyebrows. "It's unfortunate that I couldn't be here to greet you yesterday. Perhaps you didn't know, but this is my study, and no one comes in here without my permission."

He set the camera on his desk and reached for a paper.

"I'm sorry!"

Before he could see the embarrassment on her face, she scurried out, down the hall, and into her room.

She flopped into the blue chair. Uncle Nate, of all people! She had blundered into his private study—the last thing she wanted to do—and what would he think of her now?

All because of the sea otter! Karin was the one who had taken her there. She must have done it on purpose.

The knowledge came like a cold breath along her skin. She remembered how quickly her cousin had disappeared, and her chilly feeling was replaced by a flush of anger. Well! The friend she'd hoped to find on Bartlett Island certainly wouldn't be Karin Fletcher.

A *chrr chrr chrr* sounded outside, and she wandered over to her window to watch the scolding squirrel. The black dog was watching too, and she remembered her plan to visit him. At least he didn't have any bad opinions of her.

First, she'd better tidy up. She stuffed her pajamas under her pillow and smoothed the comforter in case Aunt Myra checked the room, like her stepmom would.

The long blue drapes at the end of the room slid open easily, and she discovered another window and a glass door leading to a balcony. The door was locked, but the balcony had trees hanging over it, and it looked like a good place to read. Maybe Aunt Myra would let her have the key.

She gave the room a quick glance and hurried downstairs to make friends with the dog.

"Siem." She said his name gently and walked toward him with her hand held flat and low, the way her brother had taught her. The dog lifted his

23

head and stared at her with golden eyes. "Easy, boy," she said. "I want to be your friend."

Siem rose, took a few steps forward, and sniffed at her outstretched hand. The glossy black head reached as high as her waist, and she said, "You're kind of big, aren't you? I'm glad you decided to be nice."

She scratched behind his ears. "Do you want to show me around?" she said. "Where's the beach?"

The dog looked toward the ocean, and she followed him through more cedar trees to a place where stones had been set into the bank, forming rough stair steps down to the beach.

She paused to gaze at the shining, dancing blue spread below. The smell of the sea drifted up, sharp and exciting, pulling her down the steps to the sloping brown shelves of rock that made up the beach. The only sand here was in the bottom of small pools that glistened in the rocks.

She kicked off her sandals beside a driftwood log and walked down to the ocean to let ice-cold ripples break over her feet. Siem paddled in the shallows for a few minutes but soon left the water and trotted purposefully away across the rocks.

She hurried to put on her sandals and follow him. When she caught up, he had swerved into the trees and was snuffling down a narrow trail. She walked after him, wondering where he would take her.

The ocean flashed and glittered beyond the leafy branches, and she paused for another look.

As she turned back to the trail, she saw a boy passing through the forest—an Indian, judging from his light brown skin and black hair. He was about her height, but solid and muscular, and perhaps a year older.

She attempted a shy smile, but he stared at her, his bright eyes aloof. A chipmunk ran across the trail and made her jump. When she looked up, the boy had disappeared.

Siem kept on, trotting farther and farther into the trees, and finally she glanced at her watch. They'd been walking for quite a while, and it must be close to lunch time.

She'd better not to take a chance on upsetting Aunt Myra by being late. Would Uncle Nate be there? Had he told Aunt Myra about finding her in his study?

Reluctantly she called to Siem and turned back down the trail.

Uncle Nate did not appear at lunch, and she felt a twinge of relief—at least the moment of facing him could be postponed.

But Aunt Myra began to scold her for disturbing her uncle that morning, and she lowered her head, frowning at the salad on her plate to keep from showing how awful she felt. Really, she hadn't done anything so terrible, had she?

While her aunt was still talking, she stole a glance at Karin. From the look of smug satisfaction on her cousin's face, she guessed that Karin was the one who'd told Aunt Myra what happened. And she'd probably made it seem worse than it really was.

Julie's indignation boiled over. She pushed her chair back from the table and stood up, and Aunt Myra's eyebrows arched in surprise.

"It's her fault," she cried, waving her fork at Karin. "She did it on purpose so I'd get in trouble."

She threw down her fork and ran from the table. She rushed up to her room, banging the door shut behind her, and tumbled onto the bed.

It was starting all over again. The same horrible, left-out feeling she'd had when Dad married Barbara. No one wanted her here, either—they wouldn't even give her a chance to fit in.

And as usual, she'd made everything worse.

The hot anger began to seep away, leaving a cold, hard knot twisted in the pit of her stomach.

She buried her face in the pillow and felt the little sea otter pressing against her throat. A quick memory filled her mind—Dad saying, "You'll do fine, Julie. I know I'll be proud of you."

Dad would be disappointed, but there was nothing she could do about it. Aunt Myra wasn't going to let her stay, not now. Not that she wanted to. How could she stand even the three weeks until she could leave? Three weeks until she had to go to camp.

She closed her eyes and concentrated on listening to the muffled rhythm of waves on the beach. At least there was the ocean. And Siem. He seemed like a friend already, better than Karin would have been.

She tightened her lips. She wouldn't let them know how much it mattered, how much she wanted to be part of this family. She would be cool and correct and unfriendly, just as they were. And she would enjoy Siem and the island for these three weeks, in spite of them all.

That night at supper, she followed her plan. Although her heart thudded when her uncle strode into the dining room and took his place at the head of the table, she kept her face expressionless. He spoke pleasantly to her and she began to relax, but even so, she said nothing.

As they ate, Aunt Myra prodded Uncle Nate into a few short sentences about the missing raven club, but he looked as if his thoughts were far away.

Karin threw her a sharp, curious glance, and she stared icily back.

Having missed most of her lunch, she was hungrier than ever. Now that she could stop worrying about Uncle Nate, she found that broiled salmon tasted delicious, and so did Aunt Myra's fresh rhubarb pie.

After supper, she avoided talking to anyone and slipped into the library to find a supply of books for her room. She chose several mysteries, a story about Queen Elizabeth, and a book for identifying birds.

The only birds she really knew were the sparrows and starlings she'd seen in Chicago. Here, the forest seemed alive with all kind of birds, and in the morning they filled her room with cheerful songs.

When she'd finished arranging her books, she eyed her trunk, still waiting to be unpacked. She'd better do some of it, or Aunt Myra would be sure to comment on her wrinkled blouses.

She flipped the trunk open and lifted out her swimsuit. A gleam of red leather caught her eye, and she snatched up her new Bible—a gift from Melissa.

"I want to show you my favorite verse," Melissa had said. "Here, in the book of John."

Julie turned the pages, looking for the verse. It was in the New Testament, she remembered.

She found the book of John, and there was the verse, marked with Melissa's red pencil.

For God so loved the world, that He gave His only begotten Son, that whosoever believeth in Him should not perish, but have everlasting life.

Melissa had told her to read it any time she felt sad and to put her own name in the verse. "For God so loved *Julie . . .*"

She leaned back in the chair and said the verse aloud. It was still true. She had decided to believe in Jesus, and God loved her. Wouldn't He make everything work out okay?

She closed her eyes and whispered her thankfulness to Him.

When she opened her eyes, it was already growing dark outside, and a breeze murmured through the trees. She pulled the drapes shut

28

across the door leading to the balcony and reminded herself to ask Aunt Myra about a key.

The small brass lamp by her bed made a satisfying pool of light, perfect for reading. Quickly she changed and climbed into bed with the most enticing of her mystery books.

For the next hour she shared the adventures of a French boy and his loyal sheep dog, but she grew so sleepy that she finally put down the book and clicked off the lamp.

Her thoughts were drifting hazily when she heard a soft thud that seemed to come from outside.

She held her breath and listened. Footsteps were padding along the balcony.

Finding Out

Julie lay tense under the blankets, wondering whether the footsteps would stop at her balcony door.

Silence.

She slid out of bed and crept behind the drapes she had closed earlier. All she could see on the balcony was tree-shadows. As she stared at the yellow light spilling from the window of her uncle's study, she heard murmuring voices.

For a long time, she waited to see what would happen, but finally she crawled back into bed to wonder about the voices. The next thing she heard was the trills and chirps of birds outside her window and the same *thump-thud* sounds that awakened her yesterday.

Remembering last night, she jumped out of bed and pulled back the drapes to look at the balcony.

As she suspected, there were no steps leading up to it, just a railing all the way around. A mass of flowering honeysuckle tumbled over the railing. That must be what smelled so sweet at night, but was it strong enough for someone to climb on? Probably not.

She studied the trees with an experienced eye, thanks to her brother's teaching. Two of the trees overhanging the balcony looked sufficiently strong and well-branched for climbing, but one of them was a cedar, which would be prickly.

She chose the maple tree as the most likely, and promised herself that she would climb it sometime. She could always go out the window if the door was still locked. It would be fun.

She laughed to think what her dignified aunt might say and sobered abruptly. She was in enough trouble already.

That morning after breakfast, Aunt Myra asked whether she'd like to go into town and Julie agreed enthusiastically, forgetting her resolve to be cool. It would be a good chance to see more of the island. Even Karin seemed to be in a sunny mood and decided to come with them. Since no one mentioned Uncle Nate, Julie assumed that he was working behind the closed door of his study.

As they bumped over the rough road in the family's old Pontiac, she saw only one or two driveways leading into the forest. A maple tree like the one outside her window reminded her of the footsteps she'd heard last night, and she wanted to ask whether Aunt Myra knew anything about a visitor.

She didn't really have much to describe except the footsteps, though. Maybe her aunt would think she was imagining things.

She glanced sideways at Karin's cool, pretty face. No, she wouldn't risk her cousin's scornful laugh. She'd try to find out more on her own.

The town consisted of a few buildings huddled around the long pier where the ferry docked. Aunt Myra headed for the general store, and Julie went too.

She poked through the fascinating variety that overflowed the shelves and tables. This mixed-up bunch of stuff was far more interesting than the displays she was used to seeing in Chicago stores. Three tanned women in jeans stood chatting by a rack of children's books, and beyond them, Stan lounged beside the fishing gear, drinking a can of soda.

He straightened up and ambled over to greet them. "Hello, Mrs. Fletcher," he said. With a grin, he added, "Hi, girls," but his eyes were on Karin.

Karin tossed back her shining hair and said, "Hi yourself. What's new?"

Stan shrugged, turned pink, and looked at Julie. "Nothing much happening around here. How're you doing, Julie?"

She was full of questions to ask, but not here, not now.

An excited voice interrupted them.

"Julie!" A blond woman—that writer—brushed past a stack of canned pineapple and almost overturned a bucket of mops in her eagerness to get across the store.

"Julie, I'm so glad to see you again," the woman exclaimed. "And you must be Mrs. Fletcher!" She beamed at Aunt Myra. "I met Julie on Stan's boat, coming over from Chemainus. My name is Vivian Taylor, and I'm researching an extensive magazine article about Bartlett Island. I'm just so thrilled with this gorgeous place and all the things I'm learning about it. It's wonderful to meet you at last, Mrs. Fletcher."

She paused for breath, and Aunt Myra's frosty smile began to thaw.

"I really would appreciate it, if you would allow me to visit you," Vivian Taylor went on. "I've heard about the marvelous Indian artifacts in your home. That would be a unique highlight for my project! True artifacts are so rare these days."

Aunt Myra hesitated. "My husband doesn't care for visitors," she said. "But maybe he'll consider it. We could let you know. You're staying at the mission?"

"I certainly am." Vivian Taylor's smile widened. "Mrs. Warner is a wonderful lady and has such interesting stories. Thank you so much. I'll be waiting for your call."

In the car on the way home, Julie thought about Vivian Taylor. The woman seemed friendly enough. Maybe too friendly. Was it because she

33

wanted to make a good impression and get an interview?

At lunch time, Aunt Myra told Uncle Nate about meeting Vivian Taylor. "She's really quite charming and knowledgeable. Don't you think we ought to let her come for a little visit?"

Uncle Nate speared a piece of cheese with his fork and shook his head in annoyance. "I don't have time to give interviews to reporters."

"She's not a reporter," Aunt Myra said. "She's a writer. And why should Lucy Warner be the only one to contribute her stories for an article about Bartlett Island?"

Aunt Myra's eyes grew dark. "Besides, you don't seem to mind wasting time visiting that old Indian. Or tinkering with your camera."

Uncle Nate's bushy eyebrows drew together into a frown that Julie recognized. "That's enough," he said quietly. "This subject hardly warrants further discussion, eh? If it's so important to you, she can come tomorrow morning. Call and tell her."

Julie wondered how that could be done, with no telephone in the house, but after lunch she found out.

Aunt Myra sent her and Karin to use the neighbor's telephone. As they walked along the rocky beach, Julie ventured to ask about the Indian that Aunt Myra had mentioned.

"He's a strange old guy," Karin said. "Lives way off by himself and carves Indian stuff. People around here call him the Old One. They say he's an Indian shaman."

34

"What's a shaman?"

"Oh, you know, like a witch doctor. He puts evil spells on people and has strange powers. Most people stay away from him."

Karin looked up at a small white house perched above the beach. "Here's where the Stewarts live. They'll let us use their phone."

After Karin had made the phone call and they were on their way back, Julie remembered to ask her another question. "Do you ever hear a thumping noise early in the morning?"

"Yes, every morning on the dot," Karin said. "He's doing his exercises. *Cal-is-then-ics,* he calls them."

"But who?"

Karin's face darkened. "My father, who else? He says his precious research job is so demanding that he has to keep in top shape. So he can work on it every minute of the day."

"You mean, when he's not there for lunch—"

"He's working. Research. The most important thing in the world to him. He forgets to come to meals sometimes. Once in a while he has to go over to Vancouver, but it's all part of that job. He never takes us along."

She shrugged as if it didn't matter, but Julie saw the hurt in her eyes.

Quickly she changed the subject. "Is it safe to swim out there?" She waved a hand at the gentle swells of the ocean. "The only place I've done any swimming is in a pool."

Karin was silent for a minute, gazing out at the water, her face still shadowed. Then she flipped her hair back and answered. "Sure, it's safe. Want to try? It's been too cool so far this year, but the sun feels pretty warm today."

They ran up to the house together, and Julie put on her swimsuit in a hurry.

Back down at the beach, she took a cautious step into the ocean, remembering how cold the water had felt to her toes that first day. Her toes had been right. This was ice water. By the time she was out knee-deep, she'd started shivering.

She looked for Karin, who had plunged right in and was swimming in lazy circles.

"C'mon, jump in fast," Karin called. "It's the only way. You'll freeze standing there."

Julie inched in a little deeper, her bare feet finding their way along the smooth rock bottom.

Siem torpedoed past, showering her with icy spray. She squealed, took a deep breath, and dived into the water, swimming hard until she reached them.

"Better than a swimming pool?" Karin asked.

"Oh, my! Yes!" Julie gasped, tingling all over. "Compared to this, a swimming pool is like a bathtub."

The dog put a huge, friendly paw on her shoulder. "No, no, Siem, don't!" she cried. "You're too heavy for me. Here, fetch!" She snatched at a floating stick and threw it as far as she could.

While she waited for Siem to return, she flipped onto her back and asked, "What do you think about

Vivian Taylor? Wouldn't it be exciting if she wrote about your family?"

"I don't know about that, but she sure made an impression on Mom." Karin bobbed under the surface and up again. "Wait until she tries to turn on the charm with Dad, tomorrow. She's going to get a surprise."

Once again, talking about her father seemed to darken Karin's mood. "I've had enough of this," she said. "I'm going in."

Julie was glad to follow her and get warm again. Vivian Taylor's visit tomorrow could prove to be interesting. Maybe she'd find out something more about Uncle Nate's job. At least he'd have to answer the writer's questions—or would he?

Mysteries

The next morning, Julie made sure she was down at the dock in time for Vivian Taylor's arrival. She would see Stan again too—he'd be bringing the writer in the mission boat.

She sat on the stone steps beside Siem to wait for them, absentmindedly stroking the thick black fur on his neck. Karin had been cool and distant ever since they'd gone swimming, as if she regretted being the slightest bit friendly for a few minutes.

She sighed. Why did her cousin dislike her so much?

The dog stiffened under her hand, and she glanced up. The boat was docking. Vivian Taylor stepped gracefully out of it and started up the path, chattering to Stan.

She caught sight of Julie and rushed forward to put an arm around her, saying, "Julie, it's so nice to see you again!"

Julie didn't mind, but Siem did. He sprang between them, a growl rumbling deep in his throat.

"Oh, my!" The writer stepped back, clutching at her camera. "He is unpleasant, isn't he? Hello, Mrs. Fletcher, how are you today?"

Aunt Myra had joined them, and she was frowning. "Julie, take that dog away from here. I wish he weren't so rude to visitors." She put on her stiff little smile. "Hello, Miss Taylor. My husband will be glad to see you in the library."

Julie left Siem out by the doghouse and hurried inside so she wouldn't miss anything. She wondered how glad Uncle Nate really was when she saw his grim face. Although he was answering Vivian Taylor's questions politely, his voice had a chilly edge to it.

The writer sounded as if she knew quite a bit about the Indian art he'd collected, but Uncle Nate did not seem to be impressed.

"Oh, yes," she exclaimed. "This beautiful ladle is definitely from the Haida tribe. Mountain-goat horn, isn't it?" She looked up at Uncle Nate from under her long eyelashes.

He nodded.

She picked up a wooden spatula, delicately carved with strange flowing figures. "What did they use these beautiful spoons for?" she asked.

"The soapberry mixture they served at feasts."

She scribbled busily in her notebook.

She eyed a wooden comb decorated with a tiny bear. "Now this is really a prize!" She reached to pick it up, and Uncle Nate's frown stopped her.

39

"The Tlingit were simply excellent at carving, weren't they?" she said quickly.

She stepped over to admire his photographs, and when they'd finished a complicated-sounding discussion about photography, she smiled at Aunt Myra. "Your husband really has a marvelous collection here. Lucy Warner said you had several Tlingit pieces, but all I can see is this comb."

She looked around the library with bright eyes. "Are the rest of them somewhere else?"

"Well, we did have a Tlingit raven club in the collection upstairs," Aunt Myra said, "but it seems to be—"

Uncle Nate interrupted. "Don't you have enough material for your article, Miss Taylor?"

"Oh!" Her pretty face fell, and she looked so downcast that Julie felt sorry for her. "Wouldn't you please let me have just a peek at your other collection?"

Aunt Myra gave Uncle Nate an imploring look, and he turned toward the stairs. "Up here."

Julie, Karin, and Stan followed them, but when they reached the top, Uncle Nate waved his arms irritably, as if he were shooing a flock of chickens. "Why don't you kids play outside, eh?"

Disappointed, Julie went back downstairs with Stan and Karin. She'd hoped for a chance to look at the rest of the collection in his study, especially the carved sea otter.

"Why didn't he let us stay?" she asked as they walked down the steps to the beach.

Karin shrugged. "Who knows? He hates kids, I guess."

Julie sat on a sun-warmed rock and shielded her eyes from the ocean's glare. Karin perched on a rock of her own.

Stan chose a rock between them. "Where on this green planet did Dr. Fletcher get all that stuff?" he asked. "The way Miss Taylor raves about it, you'd think it's pretty special."

"Those things are rare," Karin said. "He got them a long time ago when he went on a trip to the Queen Charlottes." She glanced at Julie. "Islands north of here."

"Is that where he took all those pictures?" Julie asked.

"Some of them, like the sea otters. He still does a lot of that around here, mostly shots of our island. Or the Indians." She wrinkled her nose. "If you can stand Indians."

Julie thought of the Indian boy she'd seen in the forest, and his bright, intense eyes, but she said nothing.

Stan cocked his head. "Hey, Karin," he said, "what about that old Indian medicine man I've heard of? Have you ever talked to him?"

"No, but I'd be curious to find out what he's really like after all the weird tales I've heard. He's supposed to be good at carving." Karin's voice dropped. "I want to ask him if he'll fix . . ."

"Careful!" Stan's eyes slid toward Julie.

Karin smiled. "Don't worry about my little cousin."

41

Heels clicked along the stone path up by the house, and Vivian Taylor's voice rose in protest. "I just wanted to get a few pictures!"

Stan shot Karin a surprised glance and ran up the steps. She followed him, and so did Julie.

Uncle Nate's face was set in rigid lines, as if he were gritting his teeth. "Stan, please escort Miss Taylor back to the boat and take her away."

Julie had never heard his voice so cold and stern. Her uncle turned back to the house and marched toward Aunt Myra, who stood in the doorway, looking dismayed.

"Inquisitive woman," he muttered. "Can't keep her hands off anything." Still grumbling, he disappeared inside.

Karin looked at Julie with satisfaction. "What did I tell you? He hates people asking questions and poking around in his stuff. Especially reporters. My father is a strange and remarkable man." She shook her head and walked back down to the beach.

It was hard to tell whether Karin was boasting or complaining about her father, but what she said made Julie wonder. Why was he so secretive?

That night, she wondered about her uncle again as she watched him emerge from the darkened trees with Siem, a black shadow at his side. She'd been leaning on the windowsill, looking for stars, when she saw the two of them.

Her uncle paused by the doghouse and murmured to Siem for a moment before walking

42

into the kitchen. She heard his light footsteps on the stairs, and then the creak of his study door as it closed.

Where would Uncle Nate go, out in the forest at night? Could he have been visiting that strange Indian they called the Old One?

She was just picking up her book when she heard a muffled thud on the balcony—like she'd heard the night before. Silently she slid behind the long drapes.

As she peered through the glass, the soft hoot of an owl floated on the night air. Someone was standing at the balcony door that led into her uncle's study. The Indian boy! He held something in his hands that might be a book.

If only she had the key to this door! Could she get the window open? Silently she struggled to raise the heavy wooden window. At last she got it halfway up and reached for a chair to stand on.

Crash! The window slammed down with an alarming amount of noise.

She snatched another quick look outside. The boy had disappeared.

And Aunt Myra would probably be up here any minute to find out what had happened.

She scrambled into bed with guilty haste, trying to ignore the voices from Uncle Nate's study. Their soft murmur went on far into the night.

The next morning, she remembered the window incident right away and began to worry. Who might have heard it slam closed last night? Uncle Nate probably knew exactly what had happened.

On her way downstairs she tiptoed past the open door of his study. She'd almost reached the stairs when he called, "Julie, please come here."

She drew a quick breath and walked in reluctantly. Her uncle stood with his back to her, staring out the window. Anxiety tightened her stomach as she waited for him to speak.

Finally he swung around, but his blue eyes weren't angry.

"You seem to be interested in my Indian things," he said.

She felt herself flushing as she thought of her first encounter with him, but he didn't seem to notice. He walked to the shelves beside her, took down a black totem pole, and put it into her hands. "This is one of my favorites."

She ran her fingers over the silky black surface in wonderment.

"It's carved out of argilite," he said, "a kind of stone the Haida Indians used. See the bird on top? That is Thunderbird, perched on the head of Grizzly Bear, who in turn is holding Beaver. It tells an old, old story about those three."

He put it back on the shelf beside a smaller black totem that was topped with the grinning face of a wolf.

Next, he handed her a whale that was carved of dark, smooth wood. "See this? It looks like an ordinary whale with a handle," he said. "But try shaking it."

She held it by its curved tail and when she shook it gently, she heard a dry, gravelly sound. She smiled. "A rattle!"

"Right," he said. "The Indians used rattles like this at feasts, or for dancing or singing. They used those masks, too." He pointed to a row of beak-nosed masks hanging above the shelves.

She couldn't help shuddering at the devilish-looking expressions on the masks. With their bristling hair and toothy grins, they seemed to glare down at her.

As she turned away, she noticed a familiar face on the highest shelf. But her uncle was sitting down at his desk, and he motioned her into the chair beside it.

"I want to tell you about someone," he said. "He's an Indian boy you may have seen around here, although you probably don't know his name because he's shy. His mother does weaving, and he works part-time to help out. His father's dead, and they have barely enough money for their needs."

Her uncle leaned forward, his face grave. "Some people think all Indians are worthless, but I don't. I think they're like white people—some are better than others. This boy, Robert Greystone, is one of the brightest kids I've ever known. He wants to be a doctor, and I intend to help him in any way I can."

He paused, glancing out at the balcony, and Julie knew what he would say next. "Robert comes to me at night for tutoring. He's studying for medical school—subjects the local high school can't

45

give him. He's working hard and doing very well. You may have heard him in here at night, and I wanted to tell you about it, so you'd understand."

Uncle Nate hesitated for a fraction of a second. "If your aunt knew about this, it would worry her. I'd rather you didn't discuss it with anyone except me."

At Julie's quick nod, he smiled, a quiet smile that lit up his blue eyes, and he stood to his feet.

"Thank you, Uncle Nate," she said, and stood up too.

She glanced once more at the top shelf as she crossed the room and hurried out of the study. She had to check out what she had seen, right away.

Melissa's Letter

Back in her room, Julie pulled the small otter pendant out from under her blouse. She studied its tiny face and forepaws, comparing it with the large sea otter she'd seen on Uncle Nate's top shelf.

They looked much alike, although the eyes of the large otter weren't shut—they were wide open and shining.

She smoothed the polished wood. Both carvings had a graceful curve to their turned-up flippers. But there was something else. She frowned, trying to remember. Something else was different about that large otter. If she could get back into the study to take a closer look at it . . .

She shook her head. Didn't she have enough problems without sneaking into Uncle Nate's study?

But one thing she was sure of—both otters had the same satisfied, secretive expression. They must have been made by the same person.

47

When her father had given her the pendant, he told her something about the man who carved it. Paul Edenshaw was his name, and he lived down by the Indian village.

Dad's face glowed when he talked about the man and his carvings. "Paul would be a real friend to you if you ever needed one," he said. "He's a person you could trust."

She stared out of her window into the cedar branches. It would be nice to know someone like that. Maybe she could find out where Paul Edenshaw lived. If he still lived here—if he were still alive—he must be pretty old by now.

An excited yip from Siem, who had treed a squirrel below her window, reminded her that she'd wanted to go back to the beach. How could she stay in this room with the whole beautiful island waiting for her outside?

Down on the rocks, she watched the waves roll in and thought about Robert Greystone. He sounded like an unusual person. How would it feel to have no father? Or to have one as mysterious as Karin's?

She wouldn't trade her own father for either of them. Dad had been away a lot lately, but this fall his lecture tour would be over, and they could settle down together as a family. Or could they? Barbara would still be there.

No! Stop worrying about Barbara.

"Siem!" she called. "C'mon, boy—let's go for a walk."

As she scrambled across the rocks with the dog, she wondered briefly where Karin had gone. The girl was always riding off on her bike or disappearing into her room. At least she seemed to be resigned to Julie's presence. Maybe there was still a chance they could become friends.

She followed Siem farther down the shore than she'd ever gone before. She paused at the top of an especially large rock and discovered that it hung over a small white beach that was only a few feet wide. She jumped down to investigate.

The beach curved in a crescent shape, carpeted with oyster-shell fragments that had been crushed by the waves and bleached white by the sun. There was just room for her to sit down. She leaned back against the warm rock, kicked off her sandals, and slid her feet into the lapping sea. Even the water felt warmer here.

She lost track of time, gazing out at the ocean, keeping her mind quiet, until a robin trilled in the trees nearby. The joyous sound reminded her of the light in Uncle Nate's eyes when he talked about Robert Greystone.

She trickled a handful of white fragments through her fingers. Her uncle had his good points. Although he was so immersed in his work and didn't smile much, he had a gentleness about him, and a strength she admired.

The robin trilled again, wavelets rippled across her feet, and she realized that she was beginning to love this island. If it weren't for Karin, she probably wouldn't mind if they let her stay all summer.

The way things stood now, though, she'd be leaving in three weeks—no, two weeks. The first week was almost over, and tomorrow was Sunday.

Stan had invited her to come to church. If only the whole family would go! Funny, how she used to think church was pretty dull.

She lifted her head to follow the soaring flight of a gull and noticed that the sun stood straight overhead. Noon! Why had she forgotten her watch? She was going to be late for lunch, and her aunt was particular about being on time.

Promising herself that she'd come back, she hurriedly scaled the rock and rushed down the beach.

Sure enough, Aunt Myra was upset when she arrived panting, windblown, and ten minutes late.

Karin looked smug as Aunt Myra delivered a scolding, and as soon as Aunt Myra turned away, she murmured, "Tut, tut, Cousin Julie. Where *have* you been?"

Julie reached for her water glass, shaking with anger, and couldn't help overturning it across Karin's sandwich.

Her cousin jerked back with a shriek—quite a satisfying reaction.

Julie tried to look repentant. She threw her napkin into the puddle on the floor and helped to clean up the mess and didn't say a word for the rest of the meal.

But later, sitting in her room, she wished she hadn't let go of her temper. Karin had made a tremendous fuss over the soggy sandwich and would probably find a way to get back at her. Aunt Myra, of course, had been less than pleased. One of them would surely tell Uncle Nate.

She'd messed up her chances again.

Sunday morning, Aunt Myra reminded Karin to hurry up and get dressed so they could leave for church, and Julie was glad to hear it.

She hadn't been at all sure they'd go, because last night when she asked her aunt about it, she had looked vague. From Karin's annoyed glance, Julie could tell she probably shouldn't have suggested it.

When they got to church, she wasn't surprised that Karin ignored her and stalked over to join a group of chattering teenagers. Her cousin looked grown-up and pretty in her pale blue dress.

Julie glanced down at the ruffles on her yellow skirt, and they seemed childish. For a moment she wished she hadn't said anything about coming to church.

She felt better when it was time to follow her aunt and uncle into the small auditorium. Stan and his parents, both gray-haired and slender, were sitting near the front. As she sat down, she caught sight of Vivian Taylor's blond head on the other side of the room. The writer was listening attentively to the tall, white-haired woman beside her.

Her aunt nudged Julie and whispered, "That's Lucy Warner. There'll probably be a lot about her in the article." Aunt Myra looked mournful.

Compared with Melissa's church in Chicago, this one was kind of plain, with its white-painted walls and simple furniture. But Julie's feeling of strangeness faded as she noticed the friendly smiles that came from everyone who sat around them.

The pastor stood up and announced that he was going to read from the book of Mark. Aunt Myra seemed to know where it was, but Julie had trouble finding the place in her Bible. Finally she stopped looking and settled down to listen.

The verses told about Christ and His men, how they were out in their boat and a terrible storm came up. Waves started filling the boat with water, and His men cried out in fear. He just stood there, told the wind and waves to stop—and they did.

As the pastor talked, she began to see Jesus more clearly. He'd been a wonderful person who healed the sick and preached wise sermons. But more than that, He was God, the mighty, powerful God.

After the service, Stan introduced her to his parents. His mother smiled and asked, "Have you seen our carved rocks at the north end of the island?"

When Julie shook her head, Stan's mother said, "Be sure to get a look at them while you're here."

"Karin likes that place too," Stan said. "Why don't we plan a bike trip out there this week? My brother won't be using his bike, if you want to borrow it. Hey, Karin!" He dashed off through the crowd.

Julie wasn't sure that her cousin would be interested in such an idea, but when she caught up with Stan, he was leaning against their car talking to Karin, and she looked amiable enough.

He nodded at her. "It's all set for Tuesday—okay, Julie? I'll bring that bike over with me when I come." He grinned and strolled back to join his parents.

As they got into the car, Julie looked at Karin, expecting her to say something, but her cousin's expression was as cool and distant as ever, so she didn't attempt to discuss the bike trip on the way home.

The next morning, when Karin rode off on her bike to get the mail left by the morning ferry, Julie was glad to see her go.

Her cousin had been sullenly unpleasant this morning, ever since breakfast time, when Aunt Myra had started worrying aloud—again—about the missing raven club. Finally Karin had jumped up and slammed out of the kitchen, leaving Julie with her despondent aunt.

There certainly was something strange about that club. Strange and disturbing. How could a middle-sized piece of wood just disappear without a trace?

Never mind, she told herself. This would be a good time to get out into the forest, away from the shadowy house with its secrets. She called Siem and set off to explore. Maybe she would run into Robert Greystone again.

When she got back from her walk, just in time for lunch, she forgot her disappointment at not seeing the Indian boy. A letter was waiting for her, from Melissa! Happily she slipped it into her pocket to enjoy in private.

As soon as she saw Uncle Nate, she knew that the mail had brought him some good news. He'd lost his absent-minded expression, and his blue eyes were snapping with excitement. While constructing a gigantic ham-and-cheese sandwich, he announced that he would leave on the afternoon ferry to go to Vancouver for a few days.

Aunt Myra's face clouded with dismay, and she left the table to make preparations for his trip. Karin looked stormy and resentful, so Julie concentrated on finishing her sandwich and stacking the dishes in the dishwasher so she could get upstairs to her room.

By the time she finished in the kitchen, Karin had disappeared down toward the beach, and Aunt Myra had left to take Uncle Nate to the ferry.

Now she could read Melissa's letter in peace. As she ripped open the envelope, a strip of silky blue cloth fell into her lap. Absently, she wound it around her finger as she read.

The long letter was warm and funny, just like Melissa, and it filled her with a desperate longing for home. Near the end, Melissa mentioned the bookmark she'd enclosed.

That verse is really true, Julie! The Lord Jesus always keeps His promises. I miss you LOTS, but

I'm glad that God is there with you. Read your Bible, and you'll get to know Him better.

Slowly she unwound the bookmark from her finger. The bright yellow words gleamed at her: *I will never leave thee nor forsake thee.*

Get to know Him better? Most of the time, He seemed to be pretty far away, but she hadn't read her Bible at all since she got here.

Why not read the book of Mark? She'd liked what she heard of it on Sunday. She dropped the bookmark into her pocket and jumped up. She'd get her Bible and start right now.

She pulled open the bottom drawer of the chest and stumbled backward in fright. A fiendish brown face stared at her with a mocking grin. Its horrible, beaked nose curved sharply below empty eyes.

Julie looked away and took a deep breath. It was just a mask—one of those scary Indian masks from Uncle Nate's study.

But who had put it in her drawer? And why?

A Great Idea

Julie sank into the blue chair. Anger flashed through her. It wasn't hard to guess who had put that mask in her drawer. Karin again! Just because of a soggy sandwich?

She jumped to her feet. Karin's trick wasn't going to work, not this time. She'd return that mask to Uncle Nate's study right now, while Aunt Myra was still away. Hurry!

She picked up the ugly thing, trying not to touch its bristling edges, and stepped into the hall. Even though she knew the house was empty, she tiptoed to the study and cautiously opened the door.

Beside the Indian carvings, she hesitated. As long as she was in here, it wouldn't hurt to take another quick look at his sea otter.

As she stepped past the shelves, the hairy fringe of the mask caught the corner of a shelf, and something crashed to the floor. It sounded as if it had shattered into a hundred pieces.

She dropped to her knees in panic and picked up two curved pieces of shiny brown wood. It was the whale rattle. It had split apart, and all the little stones inside were scattered in every direction.

As she stared at it, she noticed that the rattle wasn't actually broken. It had been made to snap apart, with small interlocking pieces of wood that held it together.

She crawled across the floor snatching at the little gray stones. They were everywhere: under the desk, in the rug, beside the fireplace, behind the door. She dared not miss a single one, or someone would find it and ask questions.

When she was sure she'd picked up the last stone, she checked the floor again and snapped the whale back together. It looked as good as new, and she placed it on the shelf with a pounding heart.

She picked up the mask from where she'd dropped it, and froze. Slow footfalls sounded on the stairs. That must be Aunt Myra, back already.

For an instant, she couldn't move. Then she darted behind the open door. She was going to push it shut, but remembered, just in time, the way it creaked.

Her aunt paused at the top of the stairs and murmured, "What is that door doing open?" She stepped into the study, looking worried. Her eyes widened in astonishment.

"Julie! What are you doing with that mask?" she said.

"I was just putting it away." She couldn't keep the trembling out of her voice.

Her knees shook as she walked over and hung the mask on its hook.

She turned to face her aunt. "It was in my room—" she began. She stopped. Nothing she said would do any good.

Her aunt was already furious. A red patch flamed in each pale cheek, and her eyes glinted like splinters of glass.

"I don't think you were putting it back, Julie," she said. "I think you were taking it. Didn't your uncle tell you to stay out of here that first day?" Her voice rose. "Didn't he?"

She could only nod.

"You've turned out to be nothing but a troublemaker." Her aunt shook her head. "I thought it would be a good idea to have you here, but I've changed my mind. You can't even get along with Karin."

The woman swayed and put a hand over her eyes. "Why does this have to happen now? I have enough problems already."

She dropped her hand to look at Julie. "Go away! Can't you see I want to be alone?"

Julie turned and ran—out of the house, down the stone steps, along the warm brown rocks—all the way to the oyster-shell beach.

But when she got to the top of the overhanging rock, she stopped short. High tide! Her little beach was completely under water.

Blindly she rushed into the trees that lined the beach and ran until she found a trail. She had no idea where she was going, and she didn't care.

Why had God let this happen to her?

She ran down the twisting trail until her breath came in short gasps. Finally she slowed in front of a tall, moss-covered stump, just off the trail. It must have been a huge tree because its trunk was as wide as her bed.

She stumbled around the broad base and crouched behind it among the ferns.

This would be a good place to hide until . . . until when?

Until her father came to bundle her off to camp? She could picture herself at camp, alone in a crowd of rebellious girls, following the rules and going to "activities" and hating every minute of it.

She rested her head against the stump's rough gray bark. She'd been hoping that Uncle Nate would forget about finding her in his study that first morning. It was bad enough to have Aunt Myra angry at her again, but when he got back and heard about this . . . Oh, that Karin!

She shoved her hands into her pockets and her fingers closed around something.

Melissa's bookmark. Slowly she pulled out the blue strip and smoothed it over one knee.

Its bright letters glittered at her: *I will never leave thee nor forsake thee.* She read the verse again through her tears, the blue and yellow blurring together.

She wasn't alone—Christ had promised He'd never leave her. But what did that really mean?

She thought about it, fingering the delicate curled tip of a fern. The verse must mean that He knew how she felt and all about her problems in this place.

Right now, her biggest problem was Karin. She'd tried to ignore her, but that hadn't worked. Somehow, she had to make peace with her cousin. Why did Karin dislike her so much, anyway?

Why not just ask?

She slipped the bookmark back into her pocket and stood up, considering the idea. She'd seen Karin go down toward the dock, so maybe she was still there.

When Julie found her, Karin was just picking up her towel and suntan lotion from the end of the dock. Feeling less courageous now, Julie walked all the way down its length.

"Karin?" Her voice sounded shrill in her ears. With an effort, she lowered it. "Karin, I want to ask you something."

She sat on the edge of the dock and looked out at the water so she wouldn't see Karin's face.

"Well?" Karin flopped back down onto the dock.

"I've got to know something. Why . . . why do you hate me so much?"

Karin stretched out her slim, tanned legs as if to admire them. "Why do I hate you?"

She heaved an exaggerated sigh. "Let's see. Because you're a dumb city girl. Because you're some relative I've never seen and all of a sudden I've got to put up with you. And because my mother says—" Karin mimicked Aunt Myra's high voice. "Oh, my! Julie looks like such a sweet girl in this

60

photo. I'm sure she'll be a good influence on our Karin."

Julie took a deep breath, but it didn't help. Something inside her tightened as if it were clenched into a fist. "You've certainly caused enough trouble for me. Your mother will never say that again."

"Whatever are you talking about, Cousin Julie?" Karin sounded coolly amused.

"You know very well what I'm talking about!" Julie cried. "You put that mask in my drawer so I'd get in trouble, and now your mother's having a fit, and I hope you're happy."

She jumped up. "No wonder your father never talks to you! I can't stand you either, and I can't wait to get away from this place."

As soon as the words were out she wanted to snatch them back, but she couldn't, so she turned and ran down the dock as fast as she could.

When she reached the kitchen doorstep, she jerked to a stop, trying to catch her breath before going inside. If she was very quiet, she wouldn't have to face Aunt Myra.

But her aunt must have heard her. "Julie," she called. "I need some help with supper."

Suppressing a sigh, she went into the kitchen. She tried not to look at her aunt's pale, strained face and silently followed her instructions for making a salad.

During supper, she tried to keep her mind on the peacefulness of her room and how nice it would be to get there. She would read all night, read until

61

she could fall asleep and forget Aunt Myra's shadowed eyes and Karin's sulky glare.

When the dishes were done, she went into the library to get a new supply of books and paused to admire the photos of sea otters on the wall.

She especially liked the one of a mother otter holding a pup in her arms. Instead of being chocolate brown like his mother, the pup had shaggy, yellowish fur. He looked so comical, with his bristling whiskers and sparkling black eyes, she almost laughed in spite of herself.

Thinking about sea otters reminded her of Dad, and as soon as she reached her room, she decided to write to him.

The letter went fine to begin with, but when she'd finished describing the beautiful island, her pen wavered helplessly over the paper.

She didn't want to admit that she'd been in trouble. And she hadn't found Paul Edenshaw, the man who carved her sea otter, so she couldn't tell him that.

She nibbled at the tip of her pen for a while longer and finally thought of describing Robert Greystone. As she finished the letter and sealed it, she wondered whether Robert knew anything about Paul Edenshaw. If she saw him again, she'd ask.

After she'd put on her pajamas and finished getting ready for bed, she remembered her Bible, still in the bottom drawer. Slowly she took it out.

She'd sure made a mess of trying to patch things up with Karin. Where did Aunt Myra ever get the idea that she'd be a good influence? That explained why her aunt seemed so disappointed in her, but it just wasn't fair. No one could get along with a girl like Karin!

She turned the pages of her Bible until she found the book of Mark. Right away it started talking about Christ and how He'd told some men to follow Him, and they did.

After she read the first chapter, she paused to think about those men—they'd seen some amazing things. She sighed. She was trying to follow Him too, but she hadn't done a very good job so far.

She turned off the lamp and went to her favorite place beside the open window. The cedar trees were already darkening into gloom. Above them, the moon looked like a slice of silver wreathed in clouds.

Her mind leaped back to Karin. Talking to her had been a great idea, but it hadn't worked. They both said horrible things, and now they hated each other more than ever.

She stood up and finished getting ready for bed. She'd just have to try harder—that was all she could do.

Much later that night, long after she'd sleepily put down her book, something startled her awake.

Was it outside? Even the crickets were hushed.

She sat up in bed and strained to listen, the silence tingling in her ears. Finally she heard a soft crunching sound. Footsteps?

She crept to her window and peered into the darkness. Once she thought she saw a flicker of light, but that was all. When she finally returned to bed, she could hear Siem, whining softly. If there was something wrong, he would bark, wouldn't he?

She yawned and told herself she was getting as fussy as her aunt, but it seemed like a long time before she fell asleep.

The next morning, she awakened at daylight and headed for the window. What had happened last night? Was it just a dream?

Her fingers tightened on the sill. What was the matter with Siem? The dog lay sprawled by his house, legs stiffly outstretched, head flung back. Something was wrong—he always slept with his head on his paws.

She rushed into the hall, almost running into Karin, who was coming out of the bathroom.

"It's Siem," she cried in a choked voice. "I think he's . . ." She ran down the stairs and out the door.

She dropped to her knees beside the silent black body and stroked one silky ear. An eyelid twitched. Quickly she felt for the pulse in his neck, and under her trembling fingers she found a slow throb. But he was barely breathing.

She looked up to find Karin crouched on the other side of the dog, and they exchanged worried glances. What could have happened to him?

On the ground behind Karin lay a chunk of something dark. "Look at that," Julie exclaimed. "Meat? Is it his regular food?"

Karin turned to stare at the meat. "No, it's not. I wonder if someone tried to poison him."

Carved Rocks

Julie stared at her cousin in horror. It must have happened last night. But why?

The big dog stirred under her hand. "He's moving," she cried.

"Get some water and a cloth," Karin said.

Julie snatched up Siem's dish and ran to the kitchen to fill it, grabbed a towel, and returned.

Aunt Myra trailed after her in a bathrobe, murmuring questions.

The dog's golden eyes fluttered open, and he lifted his head a fraction of an inch."

"Oh, good!" Julie exclaimed. "Take a drink, boy!"

He licked at the water Karin was dripping into his mouth, and after a minute, he struggled to sit up.

"What is it? What happened?" Aunt Myra asked. "Why won't anyone tell me what happened?"

"We don't know," Karin snapped. "Someone might have poisoned him."

65

She turned to Julie, frowning. "What about some milk? Isn't that what they give to children who swallow stuff—"

"Right." Julie dashed off to the kitchen again.

Siem seemed stronger when he'd finished the milk, and he managed to take a few faltering steps.

"Look at his hind leg," Julie whispered. "It's dragging."

"Yeah, looks like it's paralyzed," Karin said. "Maybe rubbing it will help. We'll keep him moving around as much as possible."

"I'll take him for a walk after breakfast," Julie said.

Karin nodded. "When we get back from that bike trip this afternoon, I'll walk him again. He'll need to rest in between, anyway."

She inspected the chunk of meat and picked it up, holding it gingerly between her thumb and forefinger.

"Mother," she said, "I'm going to wrap this up and keep it in the fridge until Dad gets back. I'm sure he'll want to see it."

"But do you really think the dog was poisoned?" Aunt Myra asked. "Who would do a thing like that?"

"Indians might." Karin's mouth tightened. "You never know about them."

"Oh!" Aunt Myra wailed. "I wish we didn't live so close to that village. What are we going to do?"

Karin looked at her mother impatiently. "There's nothing we can do. C'mon, let's eat. I'm hungry."

After breakfast, Julie snapped a leash onto Siem's collar and walked him on the shadiest trail she could find. It lay behind the house and led them away from the sea, a direction she'd never taken before.

Karin had blamed the Indians, and she wondered briefly about that. Perhaps she shouldn't be out walking alone in the forest. But she wouldn't go far, and Siem did need the shade.

She studied him as he limped along the trail. Why would someone do that to a dog?

Those footsteps she'd heard last night—Indians were supposed to be quiet, weren't they? Maybe it was someone else. Maybe it was the same person who had stolen the raven club.

By now, Siem's long pink tongue was hanging out of his mouth. "That's enough, boy," she said and sat him down on the trail. She massaged his lame leg, hoping it would help.

A prickly feeling inched down the back of her neck. Was someone watching her?

She turned and glimpsed a face through the bushes. "Robert Greystone," she said, "why are you spying on me?"

He stepped onto the trail beside her. "Is the dog injured?"

"We think he's been poisoned." She told him what had happened, leaving out Karin's reference to the Indians.

The boy's face grew stern as he stroked Siem's leg. "A cruel thing to do."

67

"What does Siem's name mean?" she asked. "It's Indian, isn't it?"

"Yes. Dr. Fletcher told me it means *respected person.*"

"I like that." she said. "He's been a special person to me, not just a dog! More like a friend."

Robert gazed at her as if he was trying to figure her out, and she chattered on to cover her embarrassment. "Uncle Nate told me about your studying," she said. "You must really want to go to college."

He stood up, his face aloof. "Yes," he said. "I hope Siem gets better." He disappeared into the trees without making a sound.

She stared after him for a minute, dusted off her jeans, and stood up. It was time to take Siem back.

That afternoon, Stan drove up with his father's truck and the bike he'd promised for Julie.

It was dented and scratched, and smaller than the one she'd left at home, but she was so glad to be biking again that she didn't care.

The road they took was a challenging mixture of pavement, potholes, and loose gravel that forced her to concentrate on controlling her bike, but gradually she got used to it. The road looped around the other side of the island, and soon she began to enjoy the warmth of the sun on her back and the deep quiet of endless trees.

As they rode, Stan asked Karin about her father's job, and she listened with interest.

"He's doing research on some kind of secret medicine, I think," Karin said. "How come you want to know? You've never asked before."

"You know that writer?" Stan said. "She asked me to help her get information for her article. She's still interested in your uncle, even though he won't talk to her."

Karin snorted. "She won't find out anything by spying around, either. My father is crazy-careful about keeping his stuff hidden. I think he uses some weird codes, too, and keeps them in a special code book."

"Does he have a safe?"

"Yeah," Karin said. "Probably somewhere in his study. He'd make sure it was out of sight, that's for sure. I guess it's pretty important—to him, anyway. Sometimes it's like the rest of us don't even exist. Like on Monday, he got some kind of top-secret letter and took off for Vancouver again."

Once more Julie noticed the edge of bitterness in Karin's voice. She felt a stab of unexpected pity for her cousin. At least Dad always found time to talk to her, even lately when she'd been so rude to him and Barbara.

Stan pointed to a wooded hill that rose from the trees on their left. "There's Bartlett Hill," he said with pride. "Has the best huckleberries on the whole island, and it's a good hike, too."

"Huckleberries?" Julie asked.

Karin flicked an exasperated glance at her, but Stan grinned. "Sure," he said. "Sort of like red

69

blueberries, but they taste lots better. They get ripe in August—my favorites."

He waved toward the edge of the road, where bushes with small pink flowers grew. "Of course, the salmonberries are good too. And the thimbleberries. Hey, Karin, what would you say the thimbleberries taste like?"

Karin thought about it, her face dreamy. Finally she said, "Thimbleberries taste like soft, velvety rich raspberries, and there's never enough of them."

Stan laughed. "Exactly." He grinned at Julie again. "Hope you're planning to stay all summer. You've got to taste the berries."

She tried to smile. She turned her head to watch a chipmunk scamper across the road and ignored a tug of longing. In two weeks she'd be gone, and she'd never get to taste those berries.

"Here's the fork." Stan turned right at a Y-shaped intersection in the road. "I'll beat you to the rocks." He sped off, pedaling hard.

Julie managed to keep up with Karin all the way to the rocky point where the road ended. Stan was off his bike, waiting for them in the boulders that lay jumbled at the edge of the sea.

"How do you like our carved rocks?" he asked. "They're sandstone, and the waves have sort of sculptured them."

"They look like giant mushrooms," Julie said. "Wonderful!"

"Yeah, but wait till you see the ones down by the cormorant nests."

She parked her bike and followed as Karin and Stan picked their way among the rocks until they came to a smoother section of beach. For a minute they stood silently, gazing out at the glinting blue expanse and the foam-tipped waves that raced toward them.

She looked for more islands, but there were only a few misty shapes on the horizon. The salt wind swept her face, tossing back her hair, and she sighed in satisfaction.

Stan strolled down the beach and Julie walked beside him, her eyes still on the crested waves. "Is it always so beautiful on this island?" she asked. "Doesn't it ever rain?"

He grinned. "Sure it does. Sometimes we get huge storms, even in summer. Lots of fog, too."

"I like fog. It's pretty."

"You haven't seen the kind we get around here. So thick you can't see a foot in front of you. Hey, I meant to ask, how'd you like our little church?"

"I'm glad I went," Julie said. "I like your pastor."

Stan nodded. "He says things so you can understand what the Bible's talking about."

"I noticed that," Julie said. Karin had caught up to them, but she went on. "I'm just beginning to learn about Christ, and what your pastor said really helped me."

"Great!" Stan's voice was warm. "I'm a Christian too. I asked Christ into my life when I was just a kid, but I've still got a bunch more to learn."

71

"Oh, come on, you two," Karin said. "Let's stop with the preaching. I get enough of it on Sunday."

She tilted her blond head and gave Stan a dazzling smile. "Let's go see if the cormorants are nesting yet. Race you!" And she ran down the beach with Stan at her side.

Julie followed them at a steady jog. She wasn't going to let Karin spoil this day.

The cormorant nesting place was amazing, just as Stan had said. She stared at the high cliff, admiring its complicated lacework of ledges, holes, and crevices. Already, the birds were arranging untidy nests of seaweed and grass among the hollows.

"They're beautiful!" she said, watching how the sunlight glinted green and purple on their glossy black plumage. Their hooked beaks looked fierce, and she was careful to stand well back from them, the way Karin and Stan did.

"There's an even better place," Stan said. "See that island way out there?" He pointed to a small hump on the horizon. "It's just swarming with cormorants and gulls in nesting season, but you have to get there by boat. Maybe we can go there later in the summer."

As Julie thought unhappily about missing that boat trip, she had an idea. She'd start a collection— a piece of everything she loved about this island. Even if she had only two weeks left, she could take it with her and never forget.

She found a shiny black feather caught in the rocks and held it up to enjoy its metallic green and purple tints. This would make a perfect beginning.

The ride back to the Fletchers' house was peaceful. She couldn't help noticing how much nicer her cousin seemed when she was outdoors and away from her family. Karin had been delighted with the cormorant nests, and when she gazed out at the ocean, her face softened.

She must love it here too, Julie thought. At least they had that much in common.

As soon as they got back, she went to look for Siem and found him down at the beach.

"Look," she exclaimed, as Karin and Stan joined her. "He's better." The big black dog didn't have his usual bounce, but he was walking with only a slight limp.

"What was the matter with him?" Stan asked.

Karin told Stan what happened, and he turned red. The muscles in his jaw knotted as if he were angry, and Julie watched him in surprise. He must really like dogs, she thought.

After Stan left, she told Karin about the Indian village Dad had mentioned and asked whether she knew where it was.

Karin looked at her for a long moment, as if considering something. "Sure I know where it is," she said with an odd little smile. "In fact, I wouldn't mind taking you there tomorrow."

That night Julie thought again about Karin's smile. It would be wonderful to visit the Indian village, and maybe she'd even find Paul Edenshaw.

But what did that smile mean? She already knew that she couldn't trust Karin Fletcher.

When she awoke the next morning, there was no sunlight to brighten her room, and her legs felt stiff from the bike trip. Gray, lowering clouds covered the sky. Even the birds weren't saying very much.

They probably wouldn't hike to the Indian village in this weather, so she took her time getting up. She read a little farther in the book of Mark and wrote out Melissa's verse so she could remember it better.

For God so loved the world . . . She smiled at the words, started to thank God for loving her, and stopped. The verse said *the world.* Did that mean Karin too?

It was an unsettling thought. If she was going to follow Christ, how could she hate someone He loved?

She sat up straighter in the chair. Today would be different. No matter what happened, she wasn't going to lose her temper with Karin.

By the time Julie went downstairs, her cousin was eating pancakes and looking impatient. "You almost ready to go?" she asked.

"I'll hurry," Julie promised. She couldn't admit that she'd thought bad weather would keep them indoors, so she ate her pancakes quickly and made sure she was ready when Karin started out the door.

Karin headed for the trail where Julie had walked Siem the day before. Today it seemed to be hung with cold shadows, and she wished the dog were trotting beside her, but Karin had ordered him to stay home and rest.

Her cousin seemed to be thinking about something else, so Julie didn't try talking to her. Perhaps today, for once, they could do something together without a quarrel.

The trail wound on and on through the forest, and as Julie began to wonder how far they were going, it ended in a large, ragged clearing.

"There's your Indian village," Karin said.

Julie stared at a huddle of ramshackle huts with blank, broken windows and sagging doors. Rusted cans and bedsprings poked through the weeds that choked the clearing.

"But it's deserted!" she cried. "Where is everybody? You said—"

"I said I'd take you to the Indian village your father told you about," Karin said. "From the way you described it, I knew it had to be this one. That was a long time ago. Since he was here, the Indians just up and left."

"But . . . why?" Julie gazed across the empty settlement.

"Probably some kind of disease came through." Karin shrugged. "Who knows why Indians do things, anyway? They built a new village on the other side of the point from our place."

Julie couldn't take her eyes off the tattered shacks. "It doesn't even look like an Indian village," she murmured.

"What did you expect, teepees?" Karin said. "These Indians aren't the same as the ones you Americans have, chasing cowboys and all that stuff. Their customs are different. Like those totem poles over there."

The sharp tone crept back into her voice. "Ask Robert to tell you about them. If he'll talk to you."

"Are those real totem poles?" Julie asked. She walked closer to the carved wooden posts.

Their odd animal shapes had the same grinning faces and staring eyes that she'd seen on the small totem poles in Uncle Nate's study. Some even looked like people's faces, topped with funny little stovepipe hats. But these posts were gray with age and spotted with moss. A few of them leaned toward each other, as if ready to fall.

"Better not touch them," Karin said. "They're probably rotten clear through by now, and the Indians are fussy about white people handling their sacred objects. You could get into trouble with a whole bunch of evil spirits."

Was she joking? Julie threw her a quick glance, but her cousin's face was solemn.

"Come on," Karin said. "There's another place I want to show you."

Graveyard Totems

They retraced their steps on the trail for a short distance, and the light under the trees grew dim, as if clouds were gathering above them. Soon Karin turned off onto another trail, "Let's go this way."

These trees looked older and taller than the others, Julie thought, as if they were giants, the last of an ancient forest. Walking under them made her feel as small as a beetle.

Ferns grew here, some of them pale and lacy-looking, others spurting up in great dark fountains of green. Fungi, like dirty-white ears, grew on the tree trunks, and moss covered every fallen branch and stump.

Mist began to curl down through the trees, and she remembered Stan's description of island fog. They reached another clearing, and she glimpsed a bank of fog curling across the ocean toward them. Would it get thicker and thicker, as Stan said?

Karin walked silently through the knee-high grass of the clearing.

At last she turned, speaking to Julie in a low voice. "This is the Indian graveyard. You can tell the graves by the totems and the crosses. Some have one of each. See that house way over there?"

She gestured to where a rocky point of land was barely visible through the fog. "That's the house of the Old One. The Indians say that when the fog comes to weep over the graves of the dead, he calls their spirits back into this world."

Karin's voice faded into silence, and Julie gazed around the graveyard, awash now with drifting fog.

Some of the graves were marked by weathered crosses, bleached gray by the sea winds, but most of them had only short totem poles. Nearby, a raven overgrown with moss balanced on a post, his wings outstretched and his sharp beak extended.

The grave beside the raven was marked with an ordinary gravestone.

Julie brushed back the overhanging weeds and knelt to read the inscription. Only one word had been chiseled into the stone. Joseph. Beside it was the profile of a raven.

"Karin, look here," she said. "I wonder who Joseph was. He must have especially liked ravens. . . . Karin?"

She stood up to look for her cousin, but Karin had disappeared into the fog.

Immediately she turned toward the sea to get her bearings, but the water, the rocks, and the distant house, had all been blotted out by billowing fog. The trees, too, had become a gray haze of nothing.

She took a few quick steps in the direction she thought the shore would be.

"Karin," she called. "Karin?" Her voice sounded much too small.

She could hear the soft murmuring of the sea, but it seemed to be whispering at her from every side.

If she couldn't find the ocean, she was lost. And even if she did find it, which way should she go?

She shivered, staring in disbelief at the thick gray curtain that surrounded her. She'd always thought of fog as delicate and lacy. But this! This was a creeping, living thing, and its fingers felt clammy against her skin. She thought, unwillingly, of the Indian spirits Karin had talked about.

For one panic-stricken moment her attention was caught by a bear totem with cruel-looking rows of sharp teeth. Had it moved? Had it? Now it seemed to be grinning at her through the tendrils of fog that curled around its huge body.

"Stop!" She said it loudly to herself and added, "You're imagining things!" She wasn't going to fall for another one of Karin's tricks.

"Hello? Hello?" She was shouting now. "Is anyone around?"

She kept her eyes on the bear totem and called again.

A dark shape moved toward her through the fog, and she reached for a stick to throw at it.

A big black . . . dog.

"Siem!" she cried, laughing with delight. "How did you ever find me?"

She wrapped her arms around his damp, furry neck, and he licked her face.

"I think maybe . . ." she whispered into his ear. "Maybe the Lord sent you!"

But Siem was staring past her into the fog, to where a dim figure walked among the graves.

The dog wagged his tail, and a minute later she recognized Robert Greystone.

He greeted her calmly. "Yeah, I thought I heard something. People don't usually visit this graveyard."

"I came with Karin," Julie said, and anger stirred again as she told him what had happened.

His dark eyes narrowed, and he muttered, "Karin, she is a bad one."

"I was the one who wanted to come," she said. "It must have just occurred to her on the spur of the moment when she saw the fog. If this is supposed to be a joke, she has a weird sense of humor."

She looked around at the totems, which seemed to float in the shifting gray. "Do all these creatures have some special meaning? Are they sort of like idols?"

"Not idols," Robert said. "Some Indians thought that creatures like Raven had supernatural powers, but they carved animals on totem poles to show the family crest, not to worship them."

He touched the bear's wide snout. "The crest of this family was Grizzly Bear. That family over there had Raven."

He looked at her earnestly. "You know how people in the States brand their cattle to show which ones are theirs? That's what the Indian does. He carves his tribal crest on everything, including his canoe and his grave marker."

"What about the poles I saw by the old village?" she asked.

"Each of them has a couple of figures, and together they tell a story," Robert said. "It might be about some family experience or a legend." He glanced at the grizzly bear and added, "Totem poles used to be a kind of status symbol, sort of like having two cars in the garage."

As Julie listened, the fog pressed coldly against her face, making her shiver. She wanted to go home and get warm, but she had to ask one more question. She waved a hand toward the rocky point, still invisible in the fog. "Is it true that the Old One is a shaman?"

He gazed at her, his eyes dark with mystery, and for a moment she worried that she'd offended him.

He turned as if to leave, and spoke over his shoulder. "You are cold. Come with me."

She followed willingly through the tall, damp grass. She had no idea where he might be taking her, but she didn't feel afraid, perhaps because Uncle Nate knew this boy and trusted him.

Besides, she'd probably been in more danger when she'd gone with Karin into that desolate graveyard.

There was no trail, but they seemed to be going toward the beach.

They came out of the trees into a clearing with more rocks than she'd ever seen at once. It looked as if a huge bucket of rocks, large and small, had been dumped here to arrange themselves as they pleased, and they stretched out of sight into the fog.

Robert looked back at her. "We call this The Spill. It's a great spot to explore." He picked his way through the rubble, heading for a place where the rocks were stacked in layers, forming a cliff.

Soon she caught the scent of wood smoke, and he said, "We're almost there."

A minute later, he ducked beneath an overhang and into a shallow cave. The first thing she noticed was a small fire, and she hurried to stand beside it.

Robert dragged a flat stone close to the fire and motioned for her to sit down. She crouched on the stone and gratefully held her cold hands to the fire. Siem curled up beside her on the stone floor, and Robert sat next to him.

Soon the warmth began to steal through her fingertips, and she looked around the cave with admiration. Its furnishings consisted of two shelves of books, a stack of firewood, and a bucket of water, but it was dry and cozy. "This is a wonderful place," she said.

Robert glanced fondly at the rough stone walls. "It must have taken the ocean a long time to carve this spot out of the limestone. I found it by accident, although your uncle knows about it too.

82

It's a good place to study. My house in the village is crowded."

She glanced at his books. "You're going to be a doctor, aren't you?"

"Yes. Yes, I am." Robert's eyes brightened with determination. "I want to do research like Dr. Fletcher. There are many terrible diseases, and some of them are especially bad among the Indians."

He picked up a piece of wood and laid it precisely on the fire. "Your uncle has been a great friend to me, and to my people."

His words reminded her of the question she'd wanted to ask. "My father told me about a friend of his who lived in the Indian village—Paul Edenshaw. Do you know of him?"

Robert shook his head. "Not anyone by that name. You realize that the Indian village is in another place now, don't you?"

"Karin said it's over past the Fletchers' house. But I don't think I'll ask her to show it to me."

She sighed. Now her problem with Karin was worse than ever. "I don't know what to do about her," she said, half to herself.

She gave Robert an apologetic smile. "I want to be friends with my cousin, but she hates me, no matter how hard I try."

"Why bother, if she treats you so badly?"

She wondered what to say—he'd think it was silly.

She watched a thick branch glow red in the fire and finally mumbled, "It's kind of hard to explain."

Robert gave her one of his studying looks. "Try me."

"I guess it's because of Christ . . ."

He waited, and she went on, her words tumbling over each other. "There's this verse in the Bible that says God loves the whole world, which includes me—and I'm happy for that—but I guess it includes Karin too. So I'd better not hate her."

He nodded. "Your uncle said something to me about that verse."

"It's a favorite of mine," Julie said. "But I keep forgetting, and every time Karin does something mean, I get mad at her again." She stole a glance at him. "I guess I don't have enough willpower."

He raised an eyebrow. "Willpower?"

As soon as he said it, she felt defeated, and all she could do was shrug.

"You don't look as if you're listening to your verse," he said quietly.

"What do you mean?"

"What's the rest of it?"

"After the love part . . ." She stroked Siem's smooth black neck and tried to remember. "It says if we believe in Christ, we'll have everlasting life."

Robert pushed a branch farther into the fire and it flared up, lighting his serious face. "Hmmm," he said. "Your uncle told me that too, and I'm still thinking about it. But if it's true, it sounds like Christ is pretty powerful."

"Yes, He is—"

"So why do you say you've got to have willpower to keep from hating your cousin?"

84

She gazed at him, thinking it through. "You're saying I should ask God to help me love her?"

Robert shrugged. "Something like that."

He stood up to scatter the glowing embers, reached for a bucket, and dribbled water on the fire. "Your aunt will be wondering where you are," he said, taking two books from a shelf. "I'll walk you back to the right trail. It's on my way to work."

She followed him out of the cave. "Where do you work?"

"At the general store, most afternoons."

He paused to survey the rocks in front of them. "The shortest way to your place is right through The Spill, so that's how we'll go."

He climbed a boulder in one easy bound and began jumping from rock to rock. She followed as well as she could, scrambling from rock to rock, climbing over others, and crawling on her hands and knees when she had to.

Finally Robert stepped off the last rock onto a trail under the trees, and he turned to watch her with something like approval in his eyes.

Her sea-otter pendant had swung on its chain while she climbed, and now it was hanging out over her blouse.

Robert glanced at it. "What's that?"

Still breathing hard, she unclasped the necklace and handed it to him. He examined it as they walked along the trail.

She explained how her father had given it to her. "Now I'm curious about sea otters," she added. "Uncle Nate has some pictures of them, and they

85

look like fascinating little creatures. Are there any around here?"

"I think they're almost extinct." Robert handed the necklace back without saying anything more.

They had reached a fork in the trail, and he pointed down the right-hand side. "That's the way to your uncle's house. Do you remember the trail you were on the first time I saw you?"

At Julie's nod, he went on. "That one is the trail to the Indian village. See you later." He lifted a hand in farewell and walked off.

She watched him go and turned down the trail. It looked like a dim tunnel with wet, green walls, and she followed it, wishing that she was already back inside where everything would be warm and bright.

Robert had been kind to her, and she wasn't going to argue with him, but now, alone with her thoughts, she could say, *Sure, God is powerful enough to help anyone He wants to. If He wants to.*

Maybe this wasn't such a big deal to Him.

She began to shiver again. Oh, forget it!

A pink salmonberry flower caught her eye, and she stopped to pick it for her collection, but as soon as she started walking again, words began drifting through her mind.

For God so loved—Julie—*that He gave His only begotten Son . . .*

She walked faster.

I will never leave thee nor forsake thee . . .

The trail curved past more salmonberry bushes and clumps of ferns and a fallen cedar, and the words repeated themselves until she began to listen.

A sense of shame, cold as the ocean, washed through her. God had said all that to her, and she was still wondering whether He wanted to help?

She hurried on, and the Fletchers' roof, wreathed in drifting fog, came into sight.

What was she going to do about Karin?

God keeps His promises. That's what Melissa had written.

Okay. She would trust Him to help her.

"Lord," she prayed, "I can't love Karin by myself—I don't even like her. But You're powerful, and Your love is big enough. Please give me Your kind of love."

The trail soon ended, and as she stepped out of the trees, Karin's voice reached her, sounding amused. "Well, here she is, the little lost lamb come home."

Julie bit her lip and whispered, "Lord? I need You!" She waited for a warm feeling inside, but all she felt was calm.

She walked past Karin without saying a word, and into the kitchen.

Aunt Myra looked up from the stove. "Julie!" she cried. "How could you do this to me?"

The Old One

"What?" Julie said. Now what had she done?

"Going off into the fog on your own like that," her aunt said. "Don't you care about all the trouble you cause around here? I'm afraid I'm going to have some unhappy things to tell your father when he comes next week."

Julie looked at Karin. She wasn't smiling, but her blue eyes flashed triumph. Of course.

"I'm sorry, Aunt Myra." She felt an immense weight of tiredness. "I got lost in the fog."

As she started to walk through the kitchen, her aunt said, "No, no. Sit down. We kept lunch waiting for you."

Julie expected a further scolding while they ate lunch, or questions about where she'd gone, but Aunt Myra had retreated into troubled silence.

Afterward, she hurried outside, purposely avoiding Karin. But her cousin caught up with her and asked in a low voice, "Did you have a good talk with our local Indian spirits?"

"Why'd you go off and leave me? That's kind of a dangerous trick to play."

Karin shrugged. "Oh yeah, I figured you'd say a prayer, and God would send an angel to lead you out, safe and sound."

The thought of Siem and Robert as angels in disguise made Julie giggle.

"He did," she told Karin. "He sent two of them." She headed for the steps, smiling to herself at the astonishment on her cousin's face.

The rocks on the beach felt slippery, and they'd be damp, but she sat down anyway to watch the ocean. It looked more beautiful than ever, silvered and mysterious under a veil of shifting fog.

She hugged her knees to herself. What a lovely place, this island! And today she'd met such an interesting person. How could she bear to leave next week?

She jumped up and searched until she found a gray pebble worn smooth by the waves. She would put it in her collection to remind herself of this foggy day, and of Robert.

Longing rose inside and melted into burning tears. She choked them back and kept walking down the beach, warming the pebble in her hand.

During the next few days, she tried to pretend that she wouldn't be leaving. With Uncle Nate still away, Aunt Myra seemed so troubled about the stolen club and Siem's poisoning that Julie began to wonder if there was something else, some deeper reason for her aunt's worry.

She helped around the house as much as she could, but she sensed Aunt Myra's disappointment in her. It was always a relief to escape to the beach or into the forest.

Reading plenty of books and working on her Bartlett Island collection kept her busy. It was fun using the reference books in the library to identify the leaves and flowers she pressed.

In the tide pools she found purple starfish, and sea urchins, which reminded her of spiny green pincushions, and little shells that looked like cone-shaped hats. She learned from Karin that they were called limpets.

Although Karin often wore a dark, angry face and usually acted as if she couldn't wait for Julie to leave, she didn't seem to mind answering questions. Was this because she enjoyed feeling superior to her city cousin? Julie liked to think that it was because she loved the island too.

More than once, Julie reminded herself that at least they shared this interest. If only they had more time, perhaps they could've become friends.

Sometimes she dreamed of doing a great deed, like finding the missing raven club, so the whole family would think she was wonderful. But her daydream always crashed when she remembered that Uncle Nate was returning at the end of the week. Her aunt would be sure to tell him about finding her in his study.

In spite of her fears, when Friday morning came, she went with Aunt Myra to pick up her uncle. Stan was there too, talking with Vivian Taylor in front of the general store, and they both came over to say hello.

Julie listened to the woman's friendly chatter, and wondered when she'd be finished with her project.

Was Stan still helping with the research? It sounded like an interesting job, and she meant to ask him more about it, but her uncle hurried them off to the car as if he were anxious to get home.

All the way back, Aunt Myra poured out her tale of what she'd endured while Uncle Nate was away. It sounded as if Julie was involved in most of it, and she dreaded her uncle's dark frown. But he gazed thoughtfully into the trees and took a deep breath of the fragrant air, as if he were glad to be back.

She could tell he was concerned about Siem, though, by the careful way he examined the dog. "Seems to be all right now," was his only comment, but his face was grave as he put his stethoscope away.

At church on Sunday, she looked for Stan, thinking to ask him about the research job with Vivian Taylor, but he hung around with the teenagers, and she felt shy about joining them.

On Monday morning, the birds awakened her early, and she decided that first thing, she'd look for the Indian village and Paul Edenshaw. If she could find Dad's old friend, maybe he wouldn't be quite as disappointed in her.

Right after breakfast, she headed for the trail Robert had told her to follow. She'd started whistling to cheer herself up when a drumming sound echoed through the trees.

She stopped to listen and realized that she'd heard it before, but not this close.

"I'm going to find it . . ." she said aloud, and started into the bushes at the side of the trail.

Immediately the sound stopped. She stood still, exasperated.

"You'll never find him, making all that noise," said a soft voice behind her.

She whirled in surprise. "Robert, you always sneak up on me!"

"*Shh.* There he is again."

Was Robert laughing at her?

"C'mon, let's find him," he said, a twinkle in his eyes. "Put your feet down quietly, like this." He showed her how to slide her feet onto the leaves and moss, avoiding twigs, and she followed him through the trees. The drumming grew louder.

There he was: a large gray bird with a flaming red head, pounding at a rotting stump. He paused to tear out great chunks of the soft wood, using his beak like a dagger, and then resumed his energetic drilling.

"A woodpecker!" she said. "What's he after—bugs?"

"That's right," Robert said, and they watched the bird until it flew off.

He looked at her. "You asked me some questions about the Old One. Would you like to meet him?"

"Oh, yes!" Julie said. "Right now, though? Won't he mind?"

"He knows you're coming."

Robert led the way back to the beach and along the shore past the Fletchers' house. "My shortcut," he explained. "There's an easier trail through the old forest, but it takes longer."

They came to a wide expanse of tumbled boulders, and he grinned at her. "This is where The Spill takes a spill into the ocean."

She took a deep breath and followed him, scrambling her way over and around the rocks as she'd done before, and finally they reached the smooth, sloping rocks on the other side.

He pointed into the trees. "That's the old graveyard over there," he said, and she glimpsed some of the taller totems.

We must be getting close, she thought.

Sure enough, once they'd passed the graveyard, it wasn't long before she saw the house Karin had pointed out. An old man stood outside, gazing at the ocean.

"Is that the Old One?" she whispered.

"Yes," he said.

The man sat down on a rock, a commanding figure despite his slender frame. Below his thick, silvery hair, his face looked as dark as leather. They stopped in front of him, and Robert inclined his head. "I have brought Julie Fletcher to meet the Old One."

Timidly she extended her hand, wondering how to address an Indian shaman. "Hello," she said.

The old man took her hand in both of his, and she felt the strength in his long, slender fingers. "I am glad you have come to Bartlett Island," he said in a deep voice.

She stood silent, bewildered by such a welcome.

The brown eyes seemed to be looking inside her. "Robert tells me you wear an Indian sea otter," the Old One said.

She unclasped her necklace and handed it to him. Gently he examined the small otter, and the smile lines around his eyes deepened.

"Your father is alive and well?"

"Yes, he is," she said in surprise.

He returned the necklace to her and gestured for them to sit down on the rock beside him. He picked up the piece of wood he'd been whittling, and spoke in a remembering tone.

"Many years ago, when your uncle and I visited the Queen Charlotte Islands, there were still a few sea otters alive. They used to inhabit all of the western coast until the fur traders killed them."

The old man's hand moved expertly, shaping an animal's head out of the wood. "The Indians thought that sea otters might be humans wearing a disguise because their behavior to each other is so tender. Your uncle is an excellent photographer, and we took many pictures."

He touched the small otter, still cradled in Julie's hand. "Like that one, otters prefer to float on their backs, whether they are eating, sleeping, or just resting." The old man sighed. "Most of them are gone now."

He dusted the wood chips from his lap. "Will you take a message to your uncle for me? Say that the Old One would like him to tell you the story of your otter." He did not smile, but the kindness in his eyes warmed her heart.

"Thank you," she said. "I will ask him."

They walked back the way they'd come. Robert was silent, and Julie's mind overflowed with questions. The Old One was not the simple Indian medicine man she'd expected to find. He seemed well-educated, and besides that, he had something mysterious about him.

Robert seemed to be deep in thought, and she wondered whether he was thinking about the Old One too. She started to ask, but stopped when she saw Karin coming down the beach.

For once her cousin had a smile on her face, and she looked prettier than ever in a new green top. "Hi!" she said. "Where've you been?"

Julie waved toward the rocky point behind them.

Karin looked intrigued. "What? To Dead Man's Point? There's nothing there, except the graveyard and . . . Oh! Did you talk to the Old One?"

"Yes," Julie said, wishing she didn't have to answer.

Karin turned an anxious face to Robert. Her eyes were soft and pleading. "Would you take me to the Old One? Please? I have to ask him an important question."

Julie watched him, wondering what he would say. When Karin wanted something, she was hard to refuse.

His eyes were dark and cold as the pebbles on the beach. "I cannot take you to the Old One," he said. "Perhaps you should go alone. But be warned, he does not welcome visitors."

Karin flushed. "You—you savage!" Her eyes turned to ice. "You could take me if you wanted to. You took Julie. You'll be sorry for this, wait and see." She whirled and ran back along the beach.

Julie stared after her cousin, and something in her stomach turned upside down.

Robert spoke softly. "I'm sorry if this makes problems for you. But the Old One would not see her. He knows what is in her heart."

"I'm not afraid for myself," she said. "Karin can be a dangerous enemy."

"Thank you for your concern." Robert smiled his rare smile. "I have to work this afternoon, but I'm usually at the cave in the mornings, if you ever need me."

He disappeared into the trees that fringed the beach and Julie continued on, wondering what Karin would think up.

Just stay quiet, she told herself. That's the best thing to do.

96

As soon as she sat down at the lunch table, Aunt Myra leaned forward, her voice high and fretful. "Julie, what can you be thinking, going off with that Indian boy? There are so many Indians around here! You can't be too careful."

"Why?" she asked, forgetting her plan to be quiet.

"Well, they could be dangerous. And they're not decent people—with their idols and their heathen ways. They're pagans."

Julie stayed calm. "I found out something interesting about totem poles," she said. "Robert told me they don't worship them as idols. They show what the family crest is. Or they tell a story. He said—"

"I don't want to hear any more!" Aunt Myra's voice was shrill. "I have enough problems without worrying about you and those Indians. Do you understand?"

Julie bit her lip. "Yes, Aunt Myra." She glanced anxiously at her uncle. He was reading a medical journal as he ate his sandwich and didn't seem to have heard anything.

Karin would be quite pleased, so she didn't look in her direction and excused herself as soon as possible. She wanted to tell Uncle Nate what the Old One had said, but this wasn't the time.

That evening, Karin wore a brightly malicious expression, and Julie knew her cousin was plotting something else. Trouble for Robert. Or her? Or both of them?

Before she fell asleep, she thanked God for helping her—at least she hadn't lost her temper. She told Him all her worries about Karin, and reminded herself that Christ, the powerful God, would protect her.

But what about Robert?

The Wolf Totem

The next morning, Julie saw her uncle on the stairs and quickly gave him the Old One's message.

He gazed at her, nodding in his absent-minded way. "Right," he said, and kept walking up the steps.

Disappointed, she started for the beach, but on the way she caught a glimpse of Karin and changed her mind. Today she was going to stay away from her cousin and out of trouble.

She hurried back to her room, chose a mystery story, and carried it with her into the trees. She could sit and read in the hidden place she had discovered behind the old stump.

Once she got there, she began puzzling over one question after another. To start with, why was the Old One so interested in her sea otter? And why had Karin been so eager to talk to the old Indian? And what about the missing club, and Siem's poisoning?

99

She couldn't think of any answers, so she settled down with her book. Too soon, it was time to leave, but she picked a fern to press for her collection. It would remind her of this secret place and the way the ferns lifted their ruffled swords to the sunlight.

That afternoon, Stan arrived to take Karin on a bike ride. As Julie cleaned up the kitchen, she wondered about the two of them. They didn't seem to have much in common, but maybe Karin fascinated Stan in spite of himself.

She looked up. Her uncle stood in the doorway, watching her. He asked her to come up to his study, and she felt a twinge of anxiety. Was this it? The sorry-you-can't-stay-here speech?

He began by talking about the Old One—that was a good sign.

"Did Robert take you to visit him?" he asked.

"Yes," Julie said. "They were both curious about the sea-otter pendant my father gave me."

Her uncle looked at her knowingly. He took a small object from the top drawer of his desk and dropped it into her hand. She stared at the small wooden carving. "It's just like mine!"

"That's right. When your father and I were boys, our great friend was a man named Paul Edenshaw."

She leaned forward. Maybe now she would find out.

"Paul was very talented, the descendant of a famous Haida artist. We often went to visit him, and he carved a small sea otter for each of us. He left the island for a while and returned several years ago to live by himself."

"He's still living here?"

"Yes. The Indians hold him in such high respect that for a long time they have simply called him the Old One. I don't think even Robert knows his real name." Her uncle's eyes twinkled. "I believe you've already met Paul Edenshaw."

Julie laughed. She'd found him at last! No wonder the old Indian had asked about Dad.

She glanced up at the large otter on the shelf above them. "Did he carve that one too? It seems to have the same sort of face."

"Yes." Her uncle lifted it down. "It's part of the story."

She examined it, admiring the way its flippers curved up to form a graceful handle. She traced the delicately-carved lines that gave it the same kitten-face as hers. But this one wasn't sleeping.

She touched the otter's round, shining eyes. "These eyes are beautiful. What are they made of?"

"Abalone shell. The Indians liked to use it for decoration," Uncle Nate said.

The otter's forepaws looked different too. They curved above its body instead of being folded across its chest.

As if he guessed what she was thinking, her uncle said, "It's unusual for an otter to have twins, but it does happen." He took his small otter and fitted it into the curve of one of the large otter's forepaws. The other forepaw was still empty, waiting.

101

Smiling, Julie took her otter off the chain, and he slipped it into place.

Now the mother otter looked fully content, with both youngsters in her arms.

"Watch," Uncle Nate said. He pressed the two small otters down against the mother's body with one hand, and twisted the base slightly with the other. It swung open to reveal a hollowed-out space.

"A secret compartment!" she exclaimed.

"Paul Edenshaw is a genius at managing secrets," her uncle said. "He made this for your father and me when we were boys. We were saving our money for a boat, and he designed it as a bank that neither of us could open unless the other was there."

Uncle Nate grinned boyishly. "See here." He put a dime into a slit that Julie had thought was the otter's mouth. A second later, it clattered onto the desk. "We'd put the money in there and of course it would drop down into the compartment. Every week or so, we opened it together and counted how much we'd saved."

He swung the sea-otter bank closed. "We never did get enough money for a boat, but we sure had a lot of fun with that bank."

He fingered the otter's chipped ear. "I was the one who dropped it one day when it was almost full—chipped this ear. I'll have to get Paul to fix it sometime."

He handed Julie's small otter back to her, and turned to put the sea-otter bank onto the shelf.

A box on his desk caught her eye. It was the size of a large book and intricately carved of the black stone her uncle had called argilite. Small grinning faces and an eagle decorated the lid, but most interesting was its shiny brass lock.

Was this where he kept his code book?

She couldn't ask him that, so she said, "Did Paul Edenshaw carve this too?"

"No, it's old Haida," her uncle said, "but he added the lock for me. You really like Indian art, eh?"

"At first I thought it was scary, like the totem poles," Julie said. "But I'm learning about them from Robert."

Her uncle sighed. "You're so different from Karin. She hates all of this—" He waved a hand at the shelves of artifacts. "And lately she seems to hate everything else too. I wish I could figure out what she wants."

The unhappiness on his face reminded her of Dad, and she felt sorry for him. Without stopping to think, she said, "Karin wants for you to be interested in her, like . . ."

She hardly dared go on, but she did. "Like you are in your work."

He swiveled in his chair to gaze out onto the balcony. A blue jay landed on the railing, cocked its head, and flashed away into the trees.

Maybe she shouldn't have said anything. Really, it wasn't any of her business how he treated his daughter.

Her uncle turned. "Let me tell you about my work, Julie. Have you ever heard of interferon or T-cells?"

"No."

"They're proteins that our bodies produce when disease attacks—part of our immune system. Doctors are hoping that they'll turn out to be effective for treating cancer."

He glanced at her and went on. "I'm part of a company that is conducting trials on immune therapies, looking for an immune booster."

His words reminded her of the day Melissa had been crying because her mom had cancer. Maybe this new medicine would help.

"That's wonderful," she said. "It could save a bunch of lives."

His face lit up. "Exactly. Trials are going on, all over the world, and my job is to gather information and draw conclusions. I take notes, and then make charts to summarize my findings."

He paused, his blue eyes grave. "A couple of big companies are racing to develop a useful drug, and my charts would be valuable to them."

"You mean someone might try to steal your research?"

"I'm afraid so—millions of dollars are involved." He shrugged. "They might try, but they wouldn't succeed. Don't be concerned. You can see that we don't have complicated locks on the doors and windows. There are more effective ways of protecting secrets."

He stood up. "I've kept you long enough, eh? I hope you're having a good time here on your visit. When's your father coming to see us?"

"Friday." She watched his face. Now he would tell her that she would have to leave with Dad.

But he only said, "Enjoy yourself!" and then he opened the door.

Back in her room, Julie watched from her window as Karin and Stan rode their bikes up the driveway. They were shouting at each other, which didn't surprise her. This wasn't the first time she'd seen them arguing, and Karin usually won.

Right now, she had something more important to consider. She curled up in the blue chair to think about her uncle's project. If he had to keep it secret in case it got stolen, it sounded dangerous. Perhaps there was a connection with the missing raven club, but he hadn't mentioned it, so she wouldn't worry.

But what about the footsteps she'd heard the night Siem was poisoned? Had a spy from one of the drug companies been trying to get into the house?

How much had he told Aunt Myra about his work? Maybe that was why her aunt wouldn't give her the key to the balcony door. If she left it unlocked and a thief got in . . .

She shivered at the thought.

Before she went to bed that night, she couldn't help feeling jumpy. The wind had started blowing, and it sounded louder up here than it had downstairs, and maybe she'd been thinking too much about Uncle Nate's secret project.

Whatever the reason, she made sure she locked her door, and she checked the balcony door and the window before she settled down.

As she climbed into bed, she remembered that her room was right next to her uncle's study with its important secrets. She hadn't seen a safe, but it was probably hidden behind one of the pictures on the wall.

The study was quiet now. Her uncle had set off into the darkening trees for his walk with Siem. Later he'd probably work for a few more hours, like he did on the nights when Robert came.

The wind still sighed in the cedar trees outside her window. Through its whispering, she heard a small noise in the hall. Was Karin still up? No, she'd gone to bed early, and so had Aunt Myra.

She propped herself up on one elbow to listen. The wind hushed, and everything in the house seemed to be waiting and watching with her. A sound dropped into the silence, a sound so faint that she wondered what she'd really heard. Was it—could it be?—a creak from the door into Uncle Nate's study?

After a moment's hesitation, she tiptoed to her door and unlocked it. Opening it just a crack, she peered into the blackness of the hall. Somewhere, a door closed softly, but that was all.

She marched herself back to bed and gave herself a talking-to. Old houses always made creaking noises in the wind—she'd read about that in lots of stories.

Right now, she told herself, you are going to start being sensible.

She rolled over and tried to think about her uncle's sea-otter bank. Wasn't it the cleverest thing?

No wonder Dad was so fond of that small otter. And she'd been right about the satisfied look on the faces of the otters. They were probably delighted to be part of a secret bank. She smiled at her own fanciful imagining.

It wasn't long before she heard the familiar sounds of Uncle Nate returning to his study and the murmur of voices.

The next morning, she spent all her time at the beach, and when she came in for lunch, she soon learned that something else had happened.

Her aunt had gone into Uncle Nate's study to dust the Indian artifacts, and she'd discovered that the small wolf totem pole was gone.

Julie's memory of last night surged over her like a dark tide.

But what could she say to erase the worry from Aunt Myra's face? She'd heard a noise that she couldn't describe, and she'd seen nothing.

She glanced at her uncle. Although he was eating his salad as silently and methodically as usual, his eyes looked dark.

After what he'd told her yesterday, it made sense that someone would steal things from the study. Maybe it was part of a plan to uncover the secrets of his research. If only she could figure it all out!

She glanced at Karin, but her cousin's face looked cool and blank. No help there.

After lunch, while Karin went off on one of her bike rides, Julie strolled back down to the beach to stare at the waves and think. How could those Indian things be connected with her uncle's research? Maybe he had hidden something in one of them, like a key.

But how would anyone know what to steal? There were dozens of things in his collection.

And how could anyone get in? The balcony doors and windows were kept locked.

What about the doors into the house? She bounded up the steps to check.

Both doors had an ordinary lock, the kind her brother would say could be opened with a credit card. Last night, someone could have easily sneaked inside.

"Julie, is that you?" Aunt Myra called from the library.

Her aunt was lying on the sofa with a cloth over her eyes, but she pushed the cloth back. "I want to ask you something."

She gave Julie a tiny smile. "If you are the one who took the wolf totem pole—perhaps for a trick or something—like the other time with the mask, just put it back, and we won't be angry . . . please?"

Julie's hands clenched. How could they think that!

She made herself speak quietly. "No, Aunt Myra, I did not take it."

"Oh . . ." Her aunt made a pitiful, whimpering sound. "I thought we'd be safe here on the island. He wanted to move closer to the research center, but I was afraid they'd kidnap him or something, so I never . . ."

Her voice trailed off, and Julie tried to smile at her. "Maybe it'll turn up somehow. Don't worry."

But she saw the expression on her aunt's pale face and knew that she'd stopped listening.

Aunt Myra was afraid, terribly afraid.

Karin's Revenge

Her aunt sank back against the cushions of the sofa, and Julie left. All this time, Aunt Myra must have been living in fear of Uncle Nate's research being stolen. How sad!

As she reached the stairway, the kitchen door slammed. Her cousin breezed into the house and soon caught up with her.

"Didn't I tell you?" Karin muttered. "Your precious Robert is in trouble—big trouble. He'll never be able to show his proud Indian face around here again."

"What happened?"

Karin smiled and pushed past her to run up the stairs.

In her room, Julie opened the window and leaned out, trying to gather her spinning thoughts. How would Karin all of a sudden know about Robert being in trouble?

Had she caused it? Probably.

An idea took shape, the idea that had been fluttering in her mind ever since talking with Aunt Myra.

Karin's trick of putting the Indian mask in Julie's drawer had made plenty of trouble for her. Maybe her cousin had taken the totem so she could try the same thing with Robert.

But how had she done it?

Oh, never mind *how.* Karin could accomplish whatever she set her mind to do.

What next? Think! Where would Karin put the totem so Robert would be blamed for taking it? Did she know about his cave?

Too many questions and no answers!

She had to warn Robert. She started down the stairs and stopped abruptly. Aunt Myra was either in the library or the kitchen. What if she asked where Julie was going?

She hurried back to her room and opened the balcony window, propping it up so it wouldn't slam down this time. As she crawled out onto the balcony, she glanced at Uncle Nate's window. Good, his drapes were pulled shut.

She swung herself over the balcony rail, into the maple, and down from limb to limb.

She'd follow the trail Robert had taken when he brought her back. She set off at a quick trot, hoping she could remember the way and that Robert would be finished with work by now.

When she reached The Spill, she knew she'd picked the right trail, and she scuttled through the rocks as quickly as she could.

111

Robert looked up from the book in his lap. "Like a herd of thundering elephants. Were you trying to sneak up on me?"

Julie ignored his teasing. "How long have you been here?"

"Just got back from work."

"Then Karin could have done it after lunch." She sent a worried glance around the cave.

He shut his book. "Sit down and tell me what's going on."

"It's Karin. One of Uncle Nate's small totem poles is missing, and I'm pretty sure she took it last night. Remember I told you how I got blamed for taking the mask she put in my drawer?"

"Sure."

"You know how she got mad when you wouldn't arrange for her to see the Old One?" Julie said. "I wonder if she took the totem pole and hid it in here somewhere, so you'd get in trouble with Uncle Nate and maybe the police, too."

She paused to think. "She wouldn't put it in your house down in the village, would she?"

Robert frowned. "She wouldn't dare go to the village, but I'm sure she's explored The Spill and knows about this cave. And she knows I work in the afternoons."

He stacked up his books. "Let's see what we can find."

The cave was shallow, and there weren't many hiding places, even for a small totem pole.

Julie poked around on the rough stone floor and behind the pile of firewood. She searched the bookshelves. Robert checked the stone ledges all the way to the back and shone his flashlight into the crevices in the ceiling.

"I guess not," she said at last. "I'd better leave. It's near supper time, and I don't want to have to explain anything to Aunt Myra."

All the way back up the beach, she asked herself: What would Karin have done with it?

As she neared the Fletchers' dock, she realized that she wouldn't be able to disappear into her room because Stan and Karin sat on the steps, talking.

Stan waved, and Julie strolled over to see what he wanted.

"Hi," he said. "Just came down to remind you two about the bike trip we're planning for tomorrow."

"Who's we?" she asked. "And where are you going?"

"A bunch of kids from church," he said. "We're going over to Chemainus on the *Sea Star*. Maybe we'll bike down to Victoria and back."

"It's a pretty road," she said, and hesitated, remembering how awkward she'd felt with the teens at church.

"My brother's going too," Stan said, "so he needs his bike, but I could ask around and borrow another one for you."

"Maybe Cousin Julie's not up to such a long trip," Karin said.

Julie shrugged off the remark, and a plan began to form in her mind.

She smiled at Stan. "I don't think I'll go this time. Thanks for asking me."

She turned to leave, and paused. "By the way, is Miss Taylor still around, working on that important article?"

"Sure is! She's going strong. She rented a boat and chugs off exploring by herself these days. Keeps asking hundreds of questions."

Julie laughed, remembering the writer's enthusiasm. "I was just curious."

She walked farther down the beach to consider her plan. If the totem pole wasn't in Robert's cave, Karin must still have it, waiting for a chance to hide it there. Tomorrow, when Karin was away, she could look for it in her room.

She stooped to pick up a white feather. Unless Karin hadn't taken it after all. In that case, the thief might come back tonight to steal another piece of the collection. Would he dare?

The next morning, Julie had to admit that she'd slept so deeply, she wouldn't have noticed a herd of thundering elephants—as Robert would have said.

At breakfast there was no mention of anything else missing, but Uncle Nate looked as if he had worked all night. His eyes were red-rimmed and his face was creased with tired lines.

Karin left for the bike trip before Julie had finished her breakfast, and the house was peaceful again. Aunt Myra poured herself another cup of tea and sat down at the kitchen counter across from

Julie, who was spreading marmalade on one last piece of toast.

Her aunt spoke hesitantly. "I apologize for accusing you, yesterday. It's just that I was hoping it was some prank, and now I'm afraid it is not." The delicate teacup trembled in her thin, veined hand.

"You mean a thief might have taken it?"

Aunt Myra nodded. Julie saw the alarm in her eyes and felt sorry for this woman with the careworn face.

She kept her company for a while, and helped with the dusting, and finally wandered down to the beach with Siem.

She gazed across the ocean in the direction of Vancouver Island. The *Sea Star* would be almost at Chemainus by now. The kids would all be chattering together and having a good time. She swallowed back a lump of loneliness. It seemed as if the people on this island went biking a lot.

Too bad she didn't have her bike from home. But what use would it be after all? Nothing had changed. She was still going to leave when Dad came—tomorrow.

She turned back toward the house, remembering her plan to search Karin's room. Yesterday, it seemed like a good idea, but this morning when she asked the Lord to help her, she felt uneasy.

Should she? Or not?

She stopped to watch as Uncle Nate ran down the steps and plunged into the ocean. He swam

115

rapidly for several yards and rolled over to romp with Siem, who paddled after him. When he waded ashore, he glanced at her in surprise.

"I thought all you kids were off on a bike trip today," he said, swiftly toweling his dark hair.

After Julie lamely explained about not having a bike, her uncle gave her a searching look, but he said nothing more, and a minute later, he bounded up the steps to the house.

Julie followed and heard him tell Aunt Myra not to let anyone disturb him. He'd eat a sandwich in his study for lunch.

After lunch, she wandered outdoors and stood, undecided, on the steps. Should she wait until later, when Aunt Myra was napping, to go into Karin's room? Again she felt that odd reluctance.

Well, okay. She really shouldn't go sneaking into someone else's room, even if that someone was Karin.

An owl hooted softly in the clump of cedar trees across from where she stood. An owl at this time of day? Or was it Robert, trying to get her attention?

Just in case, she took the path into the forest, and she wasn't surprised to see Robert step from behind a tree.

"I heard your call," she said. "What happened?"

"I found the totem pole in my cave this morning," he said. "Someone must have put it there last night. Did you know it has an inner compartment?"

"No, what do you mean?"

116

"It was easy to see." He looked upset. "The pole is cracked up the back. Someone either dropped it or hammered at it, and the compartment is easy to get into."

"Was there anything in it?"

"A piece of paper with Indian crests. It had the wolf symbol, and two others I'd have to guess at."

Julie frowned. "What could it be for?"

"Must be something of Dr. Fletcher's. Maybe a code of some kind," Robert said. "But whoever put it in my cave already knows about it."

"Do you think Karin did it?"

"I wouldn't be surprised. Like I told you, she's bad inside."

"She's hurting inside too," Julie said softly. "I wonder if that's why she tries to hurt other people."

"You don't seem to hate her so much anymore," Robert said.

She saw the curiosity in his dark eyes. It was hard to put into words what she was beginning to learn, but she said, "God's love is stronger than mine."

A sudden thought distracted her. "What if it wasn't Karin? Do you think someone might be trying to . . ." She hesitated. How much did he know about Uncle Nate's job?

"Trying to find out the secrets of your uncle's research?" Robert finished her question. "Could be. They could have copied the information from that paper and then put the totem pole in my cave. It's a handy way to get rid of it and avoid suspicion at the same time."

"Where is it?" she said. "Did you bring the paper with you?"

"Are you kidding? I'm on my way to work. I hid it back by the cave. Where's your uncle?"

"He's working. He gave instructions not to be disturbed, and I'd be scared to go near him."

She looked at Robert anxiously. "What do you think we should we do?"

Robert took a deep breath. "Okay, I'll meet you after work, down by the cave." He paused. "How about 6:30? We'll figure out what to do with the wolf pole, and your uncle might be finished by then. See you later."

As Julie walked back to the house, she thought about the piece of paper. What if the Indian crests were hiding some kind of information? It was strange that Robert didn't know what they meant, but he'd told her that the old Indian ways weren't being taught anymore.

If only she knew more about Indian crests! Maybe she could find a book in the library.

Aunt Myra sat hunched over the kitchen counter with her head in her hands. Once more, Julie felt an unfamiliar stirring of pity.

"What's the matter, Aunt Myra?" she asked "Is it your head again?"

Her aunt nodded feebly.

"Can I get you something?"

"Just that bottle of pills on the windowsill. This is a bad one, the worst migraine I've had for months."

118

Julie gave her the pills. "Why don't you go to bed and stay there?" she said. "I can heat up the casserole for supper, and Karin won't be back till late."

"Maybe I'll do that." Her aunt swallowed a pill with the rest of her tea. "These pills are so strong, they put me to sleep, but I just . . . I can't go on like this."

She stood up and shuffled away. "Julie, don't forget, your uncle does not want to be interrupted. He's working on something terribly important."

After her aunt left, Julie searched through the Indian reference books in the library and found crests for Wolf, Raven, Bear, Dogfish, Beaver, Hawk, Frog, and more. Some of them looked alike, too.

No wonder Robert hadn't been sure which of them were on the paper. She studied the crests carefully and read the explanation for each one.

But what special meaning could they have, printed out and stuffed into a totem pole?

Still thinking about the crests, she picked out a book to read, made herself a peanut-butter sandwich, and went down to sit on the rocks. It seemed like a long time until 6:30.

The wind had stiffened. This afternoon the whole island seemed alive with motion, and even the tall fir trees allowed their tips to bend and sway.

Sunlight gave the wind-whipped ocean a brilliance that hurt her eyes, and when she tried to get comfortable with her book, the wind rattled its pages and snatched at her long hair. Before long, she found herself staring into space more often than reading.

Finally she flipped the book shut and scrambled across the rocks to check the tide pools.

A shout interrupted her search, and she looked up the beach. Mrs. Stewart, the neighbor whose phone they'd used, was waving excitedly.

Julie trotted across the rocks to meet her.

"There's a phone call. Where are your aunt and uncle?" The woman's tanned face looked worried.

"Aunt Myra's sick. My uncle's working," Julie said. "Do you know what it's about?"

"Something about Karin. Can you talk to them? Go ahead up to the house—I'm all out of breath. The phone's right in the kitchen."

Julie ran the rest of the way to the Stewart's house and wasted a couple of minutes looking for the phone. Finally she picked it up and said hello.

The cool voice on the other end sounded impatient. "Will you please notify Dr. Fletcher that his daughter, Karin, has been injured in an automobile accident? He can locate her at Chemainus General Hospital."

"But what happened? Is she going to be all right?"

"She is in fair condition," the voice said. "Details of the accident are not yet available."

A Broken Code

Julie called out a hurried "Thank you!" to Mrs. Stewart and sprinted across the rocks. She burst through the kitchen door, and the silent house reminded her to respect Aunt Myra's headache.

She tiptoed up the stairs, hesitated in front of her uncle's door, and knocked.

She waited. Had he heard?

The door jerked open, and she blurted out the news about Karin.

He frowned. "Did you ask who was calling?"

"No," she said, wishing she'd thought of that.

"What did the voice sound like?"

"Just . . . like someone who works at a hospital, like a nurse," she said, trying not to stare at the glowing computer behind him.

"All right," he said quickly. "I'll take my boat to Chemainus and see Karin. I was just finishing up here anyway. Where's your aunt?"

"She's in bed with a headache. She took a pill."

121

"Don't say anything to her until I get back, eh? She'll sleep for a few hours anyway. No point in upsetting her until we find out how bad it is."

He looked down at Julie's sandals. "Put on some decent shoes and a jacket. I'd like you to do something for me."

He stepped back inside, shutting the door behind him.

After Julie had changed, she sat at the top step to wait for her uncle. He came out of his study and handed her the sea-otter bank.

"I'd like you to take this to Paul Edenshaw and ask him to fix the chipped ear." His eyes held a silent message: this was important.

"Put it in a bag if you want, but do it right away," he said. "You know the trail out behind the house?"

She nodded. It was the way she'd gone with Karin.

"Good," he said. "Stay on the main trail, then when it forks, go to the left. You'll get there all right."

He ran downstairs, and Julie followed.

She looked regretfully from the sea otter to the kitchen clock. How come he wanted the ear fixed now, all of a sudden? It had been chipped for years. She'd miss meeting Robert as they'd planned.

Why not take it with her to the cave, and go to Paul Edenshaw's house later? Her uncle would be gone for a couple of hours anyway.

She found a paper bag and slid the otter bank into it. Going all that way alone wouldn't be much fun, but Uncle Nate had looked serious, and he'd said, "Do it right away."

For some reason, this was important to him, so she'd better go now.

She picked up an apple to munch and called to Siem, but he didn't come running as usual, so she set out alone. The wind rushed through the trees over her head and filled the whole forest with murmuring sounds.

She glanced back over her shoulder, calling again for Siem. He would have been good company for this trip, and protection too. Was someone watching the house, waiting for a chance to break in and steal Uncle Nate's secrets? Good thing she'd locked the doors.

The trail wound through the giant fir trees she remembered from her trip with Karin, and she began wondering about her cousin.

How badly was she hurt? Had a car hit her bike?

A terrible picture filled her mind: Karin lying pale and unconscious on the pavement, her blond hair stained with blood.

She pushed away the ghastly image, but the feeling of horror persisted. It seemed to be part of this forest with its ancient trees creaking and groaning in the wind, its silent fungi, and the dark shadows that leaped across the trail in front of her.

She broke into a run. Escape this dreadful place! She forgot to watch for the knotted roots that humped across the trail until one of them snatched at her foot. She fell hard.

Gasping, she sat up and rubbed her bruised knees. The otter bank lay nearby, its bag torn. She hardly dared to pick it up, for fear it was broken, but when she checked, it looked fine.

She sighed in relief and fingered the slit that was the otter's mouth. Was anything inside? Curious, she shook the bank, but it seemed empty. She slid it back into the bag and started off more carefully down the trail.

At last she was out of the old forest, past the graveyard, and following a rocky trail that twisted past clumps of rustling beach grass. A glance at her watch reminded her that she should be at Robert's cave by now.

What would he think when she didn't show up? Maybe he'd go off and do something with the paper, and she'd never get to see it. It must be important, a link to Uncle Nate's work.

She frowned at the package in her arms. Had she lost a chance to help solve the mystery?

The house came into sight, and she picked her way through the boulders that surrounded it. What would the Old One say when she showed up like this? He didn't like visitors!

Maybe she'd just give him the package and explain, then run off before he had a chance to get angry.

She tiptoed up the steps in front of the weather-beaten house, and knocked. When the old Indian opened the door, she forgot what she'd planned to say, and silently held out the package.

He took it, and his dark eyes looked welcoming.

Reassured, she said, "Uncle Nate sent this—so you could fix the chipped ear."

"Come in, Julie," he said quietly.

He led her through a simple kitchen into the next room. His study?

Bookshelves, filled and overflowing, lined the walls. Other shelves held a collection of black stone carvings like her uncle's. Beside the window stood a desk crowded with papers, books, and a computer.

"I'll be right back," he said. He took the otter bank into an adjoining room, and she stepped over to read the book titles nearest her.

Many of them were what Dad called the classics: books by people like Shakespeare and Dickens. A row of books on the top shelf caught her eye. All of them were written by Paul Edenshaw.

She was still looking at their titles when he came back into the room. "You wrote those books up there, didn't you?" she said.

He chuckled. "You've discovered my little secret?"

"Then you're not a shaman—you're a writer?"

"Couldn't I be both?" he asked in his deep voice.

Julie looked at him doubtfully, and he answered with a twinkle in his eyes.

"When I returned to the island and started living out here by myself, people got strange ideas about me, and legends grew. So I let them think what they wanted to, and actually, I prefer it this way. They leave me alone, and I get my work done."

He smiled at her. "I'm glad for a chance to see you again. Your father was a good friend of mine. Did he tell you?"

Before she could answer, he held up a hand. "Someone's knocking at my door. Let's go see."

Robert stood there, looking surprised. "Julie! I wondered where you were."

She explained rapidly. "My uncle sent me here on an errand, just when I was supposed to meet you. I'm sorry I couldn't make it."

Turning to Paul Edenshaw, Robert held out the wolf totem pole. "I was hoping you could help us with a problem."

While the old man examined the crack in the pole, Robert told him how he'd found it in his cave.

Through the crack, Julie could see the hollowed-out interior and the folded paper.

At last Paul Edenshaw spoke. "I carved this for your uncle," he said to her. "The paper inside belongs to him."

Julie leaned closer as he slipped it out and unfolded it. As Robert said, it was just a bunch of Indian crests, printed from a computer.

"What do they mean?" she asked.

Paul Edenshaw looked at Robert, but he shook his head. "The only one I know is Wolf."

"Wait," Julie said. "I found a book about them—those other two look like Dogfish and Hawk."

Paul Edenshaw nodded, and he might have been smiling.

"It's odd, how they're repeated," Robert said. "We've got Dogfish—Hawk—Wolf. Then Hawk—Dogfish—Wolf. And then Wolf—Dogfish."

Julie picked up the totem pole and ran a finger over its glossy surface. "The pole has the same figures, but not in the same order. Here's Wolf at the top and then Dogfish."

She looked at Paul Edenshaw. "Why did you cut the notches on Wolf when you carved it?"

"That's what your uncle asked for," he said. "Two on each side of Wolf, and one on each side of Hawk. He's good at making up codes."

127

She waited, hoping he would say something more, but he didn't. He just stood there looking mysterious.

Robert gazed at the pole with half-closed eyes. "Maybe the notches stand for numbers."

"Yes!" Julie said. "Maybe Wolf is four and Hawk is two. Shark could be zero, because its eyes and mouth have that oval shape. The paper might be a series of numbers."

"Okay," Robert said. He took an envelope out of his pocket and wrote the numbers on it. "That's two million, four hundred twenty thousand, four hundred forty. If you put in the commas."

"What?" She studied the numbers he'd scribbled: 02,420,440.

"That zero at the beginning doesn't look right," Robert said.

She thought about the explanations she'd read. "You know what? I learned something about Dogfish. It's a crest that medicine men use, and sometimes it's used as a warning, like 'keep out!' "

"So the zeros are like parentheses—we should take them off the beginning and end?" Robert asked.

"I think so."

"That helps," he said. "Get rid of the commas, and we have 242044"

"What's it look like to you?" Julie asked.

"Hmmm," he said. "Try 24-20-44, like the combination to a safe? That's a good reason for anyone to steal it."

He frowned. "I wonder if Karin realized what she was taking—if she's the one."

Into Julie's mind flashed the picture of Karin lying injured on the road. "Oh, I forgot to tell you! Something awful happened to Karin. Someone phoned from Chemainus and said she was in an accident, so Uncle Nate left to go and see her."

"Chemainus?" Robert's eyes narrowed. "Are you sure they said Chemainus?"

"Yes, of course," Julie said. "That's where they went bike riding. Well, anyway, Uncle Nate—"

"But they didn't," Robert said. "I was down by the ferry dock this morning and heard the big discussion. One of the kids found out that the Malahat Drive to Victoria was being repaired, and they decided it would be more fun to go to Saltspring Island. Didn't she tell anybody?"

Julie shrugged. "You know Karin. She might not bother." Worry shivered through her. "What do you think?"

"That phone call sounds like a fake," he said. "Someone wanted your uncle out of the way."

She stared at him. "But the house is empty, except for Aunt Myra, and she's in bed. If someone has the combination to the safe . . ."

She looked at Paul Edenshaw. "Or maybe they wouldn't be able to figure it out?"

He shrugged. "I watched the two of you do it in a couple of minutes," he said. "Anyone with some knowledge of Indian art would be able to guess. And the rest of it—" He spread out his hands. "Just plain deduction."

"I've got to get back, then," Julie said. "It's partly my fault that Uncle Nate went off on that wild goose chase."

"You're not going alone," Robert said. "I'll come too."

She felt safer already.

"So will I," the old man said. "Let's take the shortcut along the beach."

The wind grabbed for her as soon as she stepped out of the cabin, and she hurried behind Robert across the rocky beach. Her face stung with the icy spray from wind-whipped waves, and the rocks felt slippery underfoot.

Beside her, Paul Edenshaw walked swiftly and silently.

Soon they were passing the graveyard, but she didn't give it a glance. It was all she could do to keep up with Robert.

They entered The Spill.

She jumped from one spray-drenched rock to another, made a bad landing, and cried out as her feet slipped from under her.

A strong arm caught and steadied her, but as he did so, Paul Edenshaw stumbled and fell heavily into a gap between the boulders.

"Robert!" Julie called, and sprang down beside the old man, who was clasping his knee in silent agony.

A minute later, Robert joined them.

She watched anxiously as Paul Edenshaw leaned on Robert, trying to step up onto a rock.

The man paused, his jaw clenched in pain. "This knee won't make it."

He sank down onto a rock. "You two go ahead. Let me rest here for a bit."

Julie shook her head at Robert. "Can you take him back?"

"Sure. But will you be okay by yourself?"

She nodded, not letting herself think, and turned to face The Spill once more.

Robert's voice followed her. "I'll be there, as soon as—" The rest of his words were torn away by the wind.

Hurry! She told herself. Be careful!

If only she'd thought to ask more questions when she took that phone call! She shook off her regrets and concentrated on the rocks under her feet.

Jump. Crawl. Step down. Step up. Scramble. The Spill seemed a mile wide.

She slid all the way down the side of a huge boulder, ended in a heap on the sand, and crouched there, panting.

These rocks were bad enough, but what would she find at the house?

Fear clutched at her, so cold she could hardly move.

"Lord," she whispered, "I need You! Make me strong for this—and whatever else happens."

She wiped the salt spray out of her eyes and pulled herself up onto the next boulder with fresh courage. The wind tore at her hair and her jacket, but she hunched herself against it and kept going.

Finally she was out of The Spill and trotting along the beach. As she neared the house, she tried to plan.

First, make sure the safe was untouched, but what if the thief had already been there?

What about Aunt Myra?

She began to run.

At last she reached the front door—unlocked!—and raced upstairs. The door to her uncle's study stood open. With rising dread, she looked for the safe.

A picture hung crookedly on the wall, and behind it, she found the safe. It was open. Empty.

Sick at heart, she sank into the chair at her uncle's desk. The black argillite box stood there, its brass lock twisted and broken. With shaking fingers she lifted the lid. The box, too, was empty.

Secrets

A dog was barking, full-throated and savage. It sounded like Siem. She had to go find him.

She dragged herself out of the chair, and a woman's feeble cry startled her. "Julie, is that you?"

Aunt Myra! What had happened to her?

She ran downstairs to the hall, where her aunt stood, pale and bewildered.

She took her aunt's frail hand and tried to speak soothingly. "Come, Aunt Myra. You should be in bed." She led her aunt up the stairs.

"Oh, Julie, I think someone was here," Aunt Myra said. "But I couldn't wake up . . . those pills . . ."

"It's going to be all right," she said, hoping her aunt wouldn't ask about the furious barking that went on and on.

She tucked a blanket around her aunt's thin shoulders. "You rest while I go check on something, and then I'll come back and make you a cup of tea."

Her aunt's eyes closed obediently. "I'm glad you're here," she murmured.

As she ran out of the house, she fought back her growing panic. This nightmare was happening because of the phone call. Her fault.

She headed for Siem, who was still barking that terrifying bark and lunging against the rope that tied him to a tree.

As soon as he saw her, he quieted, wriggling all over as she pulled a choking loop off his neck.

"Who did this to you, poor guy?"

As if in answer to her question, she heard the stutter of a boat's engine. Of course the thief had come by boat. Why hadn't she thought of that? She'd just missed him.

"Come on, Siem!" She flung herself down the path to the dock. The boat's engine roared, and its throbbing seemed to fill her ears.

The engine's noise became a mutter that quickly faded until all she could hear was her own gasping breaths and the sound of her feet, pounding on the boards of the dock.

She peered across the water, but it lay glimmering and empty under the setting sun. Too late. Defeat settled like a stone in her stomach.

Someone had taken Uncle Nate's papers, and now he had escaped.

Siem stood beside her, growls rumbling deep in his throat.

He grew still, ears pricked forward, listening. Julie held her breath and listened too, watching as the dog's tail began to swing from side to side.

Then she heard it, the purr of another, larger boat. It was Uncle Nate's cabin cruiser. Part of her wanted to shout with relief that he was safely back. And part of her wanted to crawl behind a tree and hide.

She waited as he maneuvered the boat to the dock and tied it up.

From the stern set of his mouth, she knew he hadn't found Karin. He glanced at her as he strode across the dock, and his voice was curt. "Karin wasn't in Chemainus. Neither were the other kids. What was Vivian Taylor doing here while I was away?"

She stared at him. "Vivian Taylor?"

"Saw her leaving in a boat, just as I came around the point. I'd recognize that hair of hers a mile off."

Julie's mind raced. Vivian Taylor in the boat? Could she have been the one who'd broken into Uncle Nate's study? The woman knew a lot about Indian art . . .

She clutched at her uncle's arm in dismay. "If Vivian Taylor was in that boat, then she's the one who did it." From the corner of her eye, she saw Robert trotting down the beach.

"What do you mean?" her uncle said.

"Someone broke into your study while you were gone," she said. "I followed the thief to the dock just before you arrived. It's got to be Vivian Taylor."

She appealed to Robert as he joined them. "It fits, doesn't it? She could've figured out those crests."

"Robert, take my boat," Uncle Nate said, holding out a key. "Follow her. She was heading around the east point. Make sure she doesn't leave the island."

Robert nodded and sprinted to the boat.

Julie tried to explain. "Robert said he heard the kids change their plans, and we realized that the phone call must have been a trick. So I got back here as fast as I could. Aunt Myra's all right—she slept through the whole thing, but . . ."

She ran out of words and her uncle turned wearily away.

They walked silently up the path to the house. She peered at her uncle's face, but she couldn't see his expression in the fading light. The wind had dropped, and the tree branches hung black against the sunset.

When her uncle spoke, it was in his usual calm voice. "Did you get the sea-otter bank to Paul all right?"

"Yes," she said. "He was going to come back with me, but he hurt his knee on the way and Robert stayed to help him."

She paused, still worried about the old man. "Somehow the wolf totem pole turned up in Robert's cave, but it was cracked, and he found that paper in it. Was it the combination to your safe?"

"You figured that out too?"

"We thought it must be important if someone had stolen it. I still don't understand how Vivian Taylor knew to steal that one, with so many pieces in your collection."

Her uncle didn't reply. He was probably so upset about the whole thing that he didn't want to puzzle over the details.

She matched her steps to his long strides, wondering whether Robert had been able to catch up with Vivian Taylor.

Light shone from the kitchen windows. Inside, Karin and Stan were busily making sandwiches, but her uncle didn't stop. He walked quickly through the kitchen and up the stairs.

Stan grinned at her. "Hi! We just got back. Looks like you've been out, too."

Julie couldn't return his cheerful greeting. "Is Aunt Myra still in bed?"

At Karin's nod, she remembered the cup of tea she'd promised her aunt. It seemed hours ago.

She filled the kettle with water, and Stan kept talking as Uncle Nate walked back into the kitchen.

"We sure were glad we decided to go over to Saltspring," Stan said. "You should see how they've fixed up the roads."

Julie looked at her uncle, who seemed to be absorbed in slicing cheese for his sandwich.

"Tell them," he finally said.

"We thought you'd gone to Chemainus," Julie said. "We . . . we got a phone call from Chemainus about Karin."

Karin glanced up from her sandwich, looking wary.

"Someone said you were hurt in an accident over there."

"Didn't Miss Taylor tell you we'd changed our plans?" Karin asked. "She was so nice, she even suggested it. She said she wanted to come back and see Aunt Myra, anyway."

"She came," Uncle Nate said. "After I left to go and see what had happened to you in Chemainus. Apparently that's when she robbed my study."

Karin turned pale under her tan. "Robbed?" Her voice shook. "And you—you left your work to come and see about me?"

Uncle Nate stepped toward her. "What else would I do?" he said in a low voice. "Don't you think I care?"

"Well . . . I just thought . . ." Karin looked away from him, her face crumpling, and Uncle Nate put his arms around her.

Julie threw a glance at Stan and they left the kitchen, closing the door behind them.

In the library, she gazed miserably at the sea-otter photos and finally muttered, "It's terrible to think that Vivian Taylor would break into Uncle Nate's study."

"I can't believe it!" Stan's face had turned red.

Julie glanced at him in surprise. "It must have been her. Because Uncle Nate saw her leaving in the boat. Siem tracked her down to the boat dock. And she would've been able to figure out the code."

She paused. "I wonder how she got the code in the first place?"

She looked at Stan, but he sat with his head in his hands.

He raised his head at the sound of the kitchen door opening, and Julie was startled to see the panic in his eyes.

When Uncle Nate and Karin came into the library, Karin was clinging to her father's hand, and tears glittered on her eyelashes.

At last she spoke in a ragged voice. "I guess I'd better tell you too. I took the wolf totem pole. I . . . I wanted to get Robert in trouble, so I persuaded Stan to put it in Robert's cave."

Stan hunched lower in his chair. He interrupted in a muffled voice. "Wait, I've got to explain something. Miss Taylor, she told me she needed help with research she's doing on Bartlett Island, so I've been working for her, digging up historical stuff, and helping her meet people."

He looked up at Julie's uncle. "I never dreamed she was a thief."

Uncle Nate said nothing, so Stan went on. "She'd seen a wolf totem on your shelf and wanted to take a photo—the notches fascinated her—and I told Karin about it."

He licked his dry lips. "I guess that gave Karin the idea of which one to take. So then I was crazy enough to agree to put it in Robert's cave, but first I showed it to Miss Taylor. Next thing I knew, she'd dropped it—by accident—she said. She took out the paper and copied down those pictures for her article.

Karin sniffled and asked, "Where is that woman now? Did she get away?"

"Robert will take care of her until I get there," Uncle Nate said.

Something was still puzzling Julie. "Did Vivian Taylor poison Siem too?"

"It wasn't poison, she told me." Stan took a deep breath and then another. "She wanted to get some nighttime photos of the house and she knew the dog would make an uproar, so she gave me some stuff to feed him."

He ran a hand through his rumpled hair and groaned. "She said it would just make him sleepy but she must have figured the dosage wrong. I guess she wanted to check the layout of the place. I . . . I should never have believed her."

In the painful silence that followed Stan's rush of words, Julie heard the teakettle whistling in the kitchen.

"I've got to make some tea for Aunt Myra," she said. "Does anyone want something hot? Maybe a cup of cocoa?"

But Stan's eyes were fixed on Karin. "Tell them the rest," he said. "Let's get this over with."

Karin covered her face with her hands, then jerked them down and straightened up. "The raven club was my fault too. I was just showing it to Stan, and we got to kidding around, and it fell."

She lowered her gaze to the floor. "I was so scared!" she muttered. "I was afraid to tell you, Dad. I was going to get the Old One to fix it for me, so I could put it back. But I was afraid of him too."

She glanced at Julie, looking almost regretful. "That's why I got so mad when Robert took you to see him. I'd missed my chance of getting it fixed."

Before anyone else could speak, Aunt Myra's plaintive voice floated down the stairs. "Who's there? Julie, are you back?"

Julie stirred. "I've got to get her tea."

"Let me do it," Karin said. "I can take it up to her, too." She headed into the kitchen.

Stan unfolded his long frame from the chair. "My parents will be wondering about me. I'm sorry for all the trouble I've caused, Dr. Fletcher. Do you want me to go with you to the police, or something?"

Uncle Nate's voice was grave. "I'm sure your testimony will be useful, Stan. I'll let you know."

"Thanks." He looked relieved. "Bye, Julie. Tell Karin I had to leave."

Julie followed him to the door, and after he'd gone, she walked slowly down the steps to the beach with Siem close behind.

At last the tangle of events had been explained, but she couldn't shake off her sense of failure.

The drug company was going to get that precious information. It wouldn't matter whether Robert caught up with her. The woman had probably made a copy and hidden it somehow.

She sank onto a driftwood log and clasped her arms around her knees, hugging them for comfort. Nearby, the sea whispered, smooth and dark.

Siem pressed up against her as if he knew how she felt, and she stroked his silky ears.

I will never leave thee nor forsake thee, she reminded herself. She'd asked the Lord to help her, and she'd felt Him there, all through this horrible afternoon. It wasn't His fault she'd been so dumb about the phone call.

So . . . she'd go to that camp, and He'd still be with her, as He promised.

And this fall, when she went home to face her stepmom, He'd be there too. She could learn how to get along with her family.

Siem's tail switched back and forth at the sound of brisk footfalls on the steps.

"I thought I'd find you here," Uncle Nate said, and sat down beside her. "I wanted to thank you for your help this afternoon."

"My help?"

He nodded. "You were kind enough to take my latest passcode over to Paul," he said. "Since you have a key to the otter bank, I put the passcode inside. That way he'd have it in case something happened to me."

Julie looked at him in amazement.

"Let me explain," he said. "When I finish each section of my work, I upload it to a secure website and devise a new passcode. Usually, I take it to Paul myself—e-mail isn't good for secrets—and he makes sure it gets to the right person."

He smiled. "But I keep counterfeit papers in the box on my desk and in my safe. And sometimes in one of the totems. The information is designed to confuse anyone who tries to rob me. Like Vivian Taylor.

Julie found her voice. "That's the best idea I ever heard of! I wondered why you went to visit him at night."

Uncle Nate smiled again—that was twice in a row—and she smiled back.

"It's a good cover, isn't it?" he said. "Who'd ever think an old Indian shaman would be connected with my research? And it's kind of fun making up passcodes with those Indian crests."

He reached down to pat Siem, and the dog thumped his tail. "I suspected that the phone call might be a trick, but I couldn't be sure—even if I'd talked to her myself. With the new passcode safe in Paul's hands, I didn't have to worry. I was glad you were here and that I could trust you."

He glanced sideways at her, still smiling. "After Paul met you, he told me to depend on you if something came up. He's a pretty good judge of character."

A flicker of warmth grew inside her.

Uncle Nate sighed. "The next segment of my work will be less urgent. Less demanding. I need to spend more time with my family."

He put a hand on Julie's shoulder. "Your father's going to be proud of you when he gets here tomorrow. But there's one thing I must discuss with him."

"What?"

"A bicycle. You can't spend the whole summer on this island without a bicycle, eh?"

Her heart began to sing. *He said the whole summer.*

Uncle Nate stood up. "I'm going to see what has to be done about Vivian Taylor. Then I'd better stop over and check on Paul's knee." He smiled at her and disappeared into the twilight.

"The whole summer." She said it aloud, and then she had to say it again. "The whole summer."

She felt for the little sea otter that hung from her neck and polished its sleek body on her sleeve. All this time, it had been part of a secret she'd never dreamed possible.

Silly tears pricked behind her eyelids as she thought about tomorrow. She'd see Dad again!

She hugged Siem, resting her face against his warm, furry neck.

She could tell Dad about the wonderful summer she was going to have on Bartlett Island, with Siem, and Robert, and Stan . . . and Karin?

What about Karin?

Farther down the beach, she caught sight of Karin's brooding figure at the edge of the sea.

She couldn't expect her cousin to be much of a friend— not yet—until the Lord changed her from the inside.

She bent to whisper in Siem's ear. "He's changing me, you know. I'll write to Melissa, and we'll pray for her."

Siem wagged his tail, and a minute later he wagged it again as Karin slowly stood up and strolled over to sit beside them.

Julie sensed that her cousin wouldn't feel like talking, so she sat with a hand on Siem's neck and looked for the first stars of evening.

144

But then she had to give the big black dog another hug. This summer was going to be an adventure, with Siem and her new friends . . . and Karin.

Books by Gloria Repp

For ages 2 and up:
Noodle Soup

For ages 7 and up:
A Question of Yams *(also as eBook)*

Tales of Friendship Bog series
Pibbin the Small *(also as eBook and audiobook)*
The Story Shell *(also as eBook and audiobook)*
Trapped *(also as eBook and audiobook)*
Catch a Robber *(also as eBook)*
The Stranger's Secret *(also as eBook)*
Trouble with Zee *(also as eBook)*
A Day for Courage *(also as eBook)*

For ages 9 and up:
The Secret of the Golden Cowrie *(also as eBook)*
Trouble at Silver Pines Inn *(also as eBook)*
The Mystery of the Indian Carvings
(also as eBook)

Adventures of an Arctic Missionary series
Mik-shrok *(also as eBook)*
Charlie *(also as eBook)*
77 Zebra *(also as eBook)*

For ages 12 and up:
The Stolen Years *(also as eBook)*
Night Flight *(also as eBook)*

For Adults:
Nothing Daunted: The Story of Isobel Kuhn
(also as eBook)

THE DUMONT CHRONICLES
The Forever Stone *(also as eBook)*
Deep Focus *(also as eBook)*

Author's Note

This book is one of my favorites, partly because I feel the same as Julie about rocky Canadian islands with tide pools, delicious berries, and Indian lore. My family had a cabin on Thetis Island, near Vancouver Island, B.C., and we spent our summers there during my early teen years.

Memories of that island and its delights gave me inspiration when I began to think about Julie's story. Other memories, like the problems with my stepmother that were often my fault, helped me to understand Julie's desperate longings.

If you want to talk to me about Julie's story, please stop by my website, www.gloriarepp.com, and send me a note. I'd love to hear from you!

I'd also like to know what you think of *The Mystery of the Indian Carvings.* If you enjoyed the story, please consider leaving a few words of review on Amazon.com. Your comments will be helpful to other readers. Thank you!

44967632R00086

Made in the USA
San Bernardino, CA
23 July 2019